a THING *of* BEAUTY

—•——— *a novel of Glen Eyrie* ———•—

a THING *of* BEAUTY

◆—— *a novel of Glen Eyrie* ——◆

Ashley Eiman

ASHLEY EIMAN

© 2016 by Ashley Eiman

Published by Ashley Eiman Creative Publishing, Colorado Springs, Colorado
Images used under license from Shutterstock
Cover design by Rita M. Tressler
Interior illustration and author photo by Alex Eiman
Glen Eyrie photo by Ashley Eiman

Library of Congress Control Number: 2016908914

ISBN: 0692720863
ISBN-13: 978-0-692-72086-8

First edition

Printed in the United States of America

TO JANE AUSTEN
You know what you did.

ACKNOWLEDGMENTS

Mom, thank you for being my first and best editor. And for thinking this book is good enough for Julian Fellowes and the BBC.

Laura and Michele, thank you for reading, editing, and championing my book.

Alex, thank you for the beautiful illustration of Glen Eyrie.

Rita, thank you for the timeless and intriguing book cover design.

Dr. Joan Ray, thank you for your honest critiques of my writing, your fantastic courses on Jane Austen, and your infectious love of English Literature.

Sheridan Voysey, thank you for encouraging me and helping my book idea take flight.

Dad, Steph, and Aaron, thank you for encouraging me to write and pursue my dreams. This book would not be possible without you.

a THING *of* BEAUTY

a novel of Glen Eyrie

Part One

Chapter One

A thing of beauty is a joy forever.
JOHN KEATS

THE CRISP MOUNTAIN AIR felt absolutely wonderful against Elsie's cheek. She took a deep, lung-filling breath and exhaled slowly. She could hear a bird chirping somewhere nearby as she gazed upon the red, spiked rocks. The mother mountain loomed overhead, its dips and contours perfectly accented by the bright sun above.

She had crept out of bed early that morning to take a quick ride to her favorite crest overlooking the peak and the narrow valley below.

"It is different each day," Elsie said to herself. "Just like Father used to say."

Elsie adored her little excursions. When life became too overwhelming—as it too often did—she would indulge in a brisk walk or ask one of the groomsmen to saddle her horse for a short ride. Breathing the crisp air, galloping up and up to the crest, cleared her mind. An hour or so on her own, and all was put to right.

Elsie closed her eyes again, blinking back tears. The air always felt different up here, more breathable, more freeing, somehow, than it did at sea level. It was an absolutely perfect day, with not a single cloud in the sky. No rain, no thunder, just endless sunshine. So unlike England, with its relentlessly gloomy weather.

When she and her sisters and mother had left for that bleak country more than 10 years ago, she wondered if she would ever return to her beloved Colorado—and her beloved Father. Her heart had ached at the thought of never returning. But now they had returned, and this time for good.

Pressing into her painful memories, she remembered the day of their departure to England. She could recall it like it was yesterday—the way the ship jolted forward in swift jerks as the tug boat led it out to sea and the sound of the horn as it announced its farewell. Back then, she had felt an odd mixture of both sadness and excitement as they pulled away from America's shores into the great, wide ocean. She had been eager to see Mama's health improve, but the cost of leaving her home had felt particularly great.

A gust of cool wind brushed her hair into her face and brought her back to the present. She sat astride her horse for a moment and let her unpinned hair dance in tendrils across her face.

Wild, she thought. *That is the perfect way to describe this place.*

Colorado was wild, and she felt wild in it. She had loved growing up here, surrounded by forests and cliffs, Indians and settlers, hiking and riding and scampering about all day.

Back in England, if anyone asked her where she was from, she proudly answered "Colorado" with a noticeably puffed chest. Most Englishmen were too polite to express shock or concern over her "savage" birthplace, but she could not help but feel validated being from somewhere so much more free and *wild* than stuffy, old England.

In the years she had spent there, she had been a fish out of water in every sense of the word. Over time she had learned the ways of the English enough to get by, but she never truly fit in the way her sisters did. But to be fair, England was all they had known. They were only small children, after all, when Mama became ill.

Elsie thought again about the ship that had taken them across the ocean. It was black with white smokestacks and a red stripe across the hull. She had shared a bed with Dorothy, who was only four at the time, and Marjory, her youngest sister, only three, was just learning her ABCs. She spent hours pointing out familiar letters on signs all around the ship. Elsie remembered that vividly, for it had cemented in her mind the fact that her sisters were too young to have any solid memories of home. And that had made her incredibly sad.

Elsie could not blame Mama, though. She had suffered with a painful heart issue for years before making the decision to move them to England. She had not made the decision lightly, and for that reason Elsie respected it. She had been devastated to leave her home, but she knew one day they would return. She just never expected they would return *without* Mama.

That was a complete shock for poor Father.

1869
36 YEARS EARLIER
EN ROUTE TO ST. LOUIS

"AH, QUEEN, THERE YOU are," her father said and waved her over.

At only 19, Queen was already the most pined-for young woman in all of Flushing, New York. Bright-eyed and well-bred, suitors came calling, one right after the other, it seemed, from all across the state.

Her father's only child from his first marriage, he simply adored his feisty girl. Her mother, Isabel, had named her Mary Lincoln Mellen, but her father believed that name was too small, too stuffy for his daughter. After all, how many millions of girls had been named Mary since the beginning of time? So, instead, he began calling her "Queen." The name seemed to stick, and after a while everyone referred to her as such. It fit her strong personality and penchant for being bossy far better than boring "Mary" ever could.

The day her mother died was a tragic blow for her and her father. Queen was only four, and losing a mother at such a tender age changes a person, as she would come to find out. Luckily, her father was not lonely for long. After her sister's death, Aunt Ellen became a permanent fixture in the Mellen home—looking after the affairs of their home and caring for little Queen. Needless to say, her father fell quickly in love with the woman who reminded him so very much of Isabel.

Aunt Ellen went on to have six children, but none of them would have a bond quite like the one Queen shared with her father. They both adored traveling, and they went on trips together often. Not surprisingly, they were on a train bound for St. Louis when Queen met the handsome man who would turn her life upside down.

On the first night of their trip west, they enjoyed supper in the First Class dining car. Queen returned briefly to their room before dessert to fetch a fresh handkerchief, and when she found Father again, she noticed a tall, handsome gentleman standing next to him.

"Darling," he said as she approached. "Allow me to introduce General William Palmer—"

"Oh, do call me 'Palmer,'" the tall man said and smiled at her. "Everyone does."

Petite, with soft, curly brown hair and a flawless complexion, Queen was at the height of youth and beauty. She could feel Palmer's fixed gaze on her and blushed slightly as she extended her gloved hand to him.

"Charmed, I'm sure," Queen shook his hand and curtseyed. "Please, do not allow me to interrupt. You appeared to be speaking quite animatedly to my father."

"I was just telling your father about my plans to bring the railroad to the far West, and he mentioned you are headed there yourselves," Palmer explained.

"We are, indeed. To Saint Louis and beyond," Queen said and

smiled coyly. "Have you traveled much yourself ... Palmer? Oh, but I do feel better calling you 'Mister Palmer' or even 'William.' Do you mind?"

"William it is, then," he replied.

"Would you like to join us?" Queen asked him.

"Thank you. I would like that very much," he said as he took a chair at the table.

For the next few hours, the three of them discussed Palmer's railroad ambitions, their traveling adventures, and all other matters of importance. Queen felt surprised to discover he had been raised a Quaker, for he was friendly and passionate, so unlike the typically stoic and reserved men of the Quaker faith.

"Pardon me if this is too personal a question," her father said, "but why did you choose to join the war? I thought Quakers were generally pacifists?"

Palmer considered his question for a moment before he replied, "Quakers are not known for their accomplishments in war, it is true; however, I could not stand by and watch as my countrymen fought for a cause I believed in so wholeheartedly without doing my bit."

"That is beautiful," Queen said and looked earnestly into his handsome face.

Later that night, Queen lay awake in bed, unable to sleep. She could not seem to get William's face out of her mind.

What is it about him that has me so nonplused? she thought.

When she woke the next morning, she had her answer. *He is so very different from any man I have ever known.* She considered this thought for a moment and swiftly made up her mind to ensure she and Father sat by him at supper again that evening.

And so they did. As they talked, Palmer began to notice the way Queen tilted her head when she laughed and the way she cared for and respected her father. He had never met a woman like Queen. Over the course of the next few evenings, he began to seriously reconsider his bachelor lifestyle and slowly started to open his heart to the beautiful young woman with the big eyes.

When the train arrived in St. Louis a few days later, Queen and Palmer were in love. Work would take Palmer on a months' long surveying trip, but before he left he received permission from Queen's father to write to her.

He wrote dozens of letters to Queen—each one contained not only eager professions of his love but small trinkets he picked up along his travels.

As fate would have it, one stop on his surveying trip took him to Colorado, to the foothills of the Rocky Mountains. While canvassing an area south of Denver on horseback, he came to a wide valley at the base of the majestic, snowcapped Pike's Peak. He recognized the peak from a tintype he had seen years earlier, but only a privileged few had laid eyes on it—not including the thousands of Indians who summered in the valleys below, of course.

Palmer spent the night in that valley, lying flat on his back with his eyes towards the heavens, with the grand peak silhouetted by the light of the stars, and he fell in love all over again. The next day he wrote a letter to his beloved, relating his discovery and his desire to bring her there to live after the wedding.

Queen and Palmer both were obsessed with ancient castles—their intricate woodwork and impressive stonemasonry. In a fit of passion, Palmer wrote to Queen and promised to build her a castle of her own, if only she would consent to leave her home in New York and follow him out West. Queen was admittedly a little hesitant—not about William but about living in the Wild West. She was a traveler, it was true, but she was accustomed to posh places like Saratoga and Newport, not dusty pioneer towns. But her love for William was unshakeable.

The pair was married six months later. Their honeymoon took them to Europe, where they toured ancient ruins, overnighted in castles, and spent lazy afternoon hours in museums as they dreamed and planned for a new home at the base of the Rockies.

APRIL 1886
NEW YORK

"COME ALONG, ELSIE, GRAB your sister's hand, please," Queen instructed her eldest daughter.

They bustled along together down the crowded platform to the First Class registration table. Mama carried Marjory as Elsie held fast to Dorothy's little hand. Father had stayed behind at their carriage to help direct the porter with their baggage. He caught up with them at the table and produced the necessary paperwork for their passage to England.

"Why can you not come, Father?" Elsie turned to him with tears in her eyes. "I do not understand."

"Darling," he said softly and brushed the tears from her cheek. "You know I must return to Colorado. I promise to visit in the summer."

"But that is so far away."

Father kissed each of his girls, lingering for a moment with Queen.

"I cannot believe this is goodbye," she cried. "I will miss you terribly."

He pressed his forehead against hers and clasped her hands between them.

"It is only temporary, my dears," he said and turned to look at them all. "You will return home as soon as your mama is well again. I promise."

Elsie felt panic-stricken at the thought of being apart from her father. She relied on him and deeply loved him. Theirs was a strong bond.

"I love you, Father," she cried and embraced him again.

"I love you, too, darling. I love you all."

CHRISTMAS 1894
LOSELEY PARK, SURREY, ENGLAND

"WAKE UP! WAKE UP, miss!" Cecile, the governess, shook Elsie's arm. "It's your *Motherling*!"

Not two days earlier, Elsie and her sisters had spent a wonderful Christmas with their mother. She had opened gifts with them and even joined them for Christmas dinner, and Elsie had believed her mother had rallied for good. But everything was about to change.

Elsie leaped from bed, wrapped a shawl around her shoulders, and fled the room. She hurried down the old stone corridor, Cecile close behind, until she reached the door to her mother's room. Elsie inhaled a deep breath and then swung open the door to reveal her mother lying very still in the big, carved wooden bed.

How very small she looks, Elsie thought. *Like a doll.*

She quickly crossed the room and kneeled down beside her mother. "*Motherling*," she said in a low voice, "Mama, I am here."

Elsie looked almost exactly like Queen—the same dark, round eyes and soft, curly hair. Despite being only 22, Elsie daily fretted over fine lines that had started to creep across her forehead and around her eyes—battle wounds from years spent worrying over Mama and feeling heartsick and lonely for Father.

Now Elsie stared into her beloved mother's eyes, sunken and much altered, searching for any sign that she would pull through. She was far too young to die, but Elsie knew the time had come.

Queen slowly reached for Elsie's face. "My little companion."

Elsie burst into tears. Her mother always called her that when she felt particularly proud of her. Or when she said goodbye.

QUEEN SLIPPED AWAY IN the middle of the night, surrounded by her three devoted daughters. After she took her final breath, the girls clung to each other and sobbed for what seemed like hours.

At daybreak, Elsie awoke to find herself in her own room. Cecile must have escorted her there last night, but she had no memory of it. For a moment, she wondered whether she had dreamed up the events of last night, but as she sat up and looked around her room, she knew the worst had actually happened.

Elsie needed to send a telegram to Father, but her feet felt like they were clad in iron chains. She reached for the glass of water next to her bed and sipped it slowly. After a few minutes, she felt strong enough to swing her legs out of bed and stand up. She looked at herself in the mirror. A haggard, old woman stared back at her.

She splashed her face with the water from her washbasin and dried it on an embroidered towel. When she peered into the mirror again, she recognized herself. Everything felt surreal to her—even her writing desk and pen. As she sat down to compose a message to Father, she found she could not form the words.

Elsie stared at the blank paper for several minutes, until she heard a soft rap on the door. It was Cecile.

"Miss?" she said as she quietly opened the door. "I thought I heard movement in here. Are you quite alright?"

Elsie turned to look at her and only nodded.

"Is there anything I can get you?"

Elsie motioned to the writing desk. "W-would you help me, Cecile?" she asked. "I need to tell my father. But I do not know what to say."

Cecile sat down next to Elsie and wrote a brief message: *Dear Father, Mama is with God now. Please hurry. Elsie*

Cecile knew their father could not come any more quickly. She had written to him a week ago to urge him to come to England, and they had received a telegram from him the day before yesterday; he was en route on the Atlantic. She rang the bell then for Peter, the manservant. When he arrived, she handed him the letter and instructed him, "Please have this sent. Right away."

"Yes, miss," he said, then bowed and left the room.

"WHAT DO WE DO now, Elsie?" Marjory, her youngest sister, said through tears.

After Cecile's departure from her room that morning, Elsie had crawled back in bed for several hours. She woke to the sound of Marjory entering her room and slipping into bed with her. A while later, Dorothy did the same. Now the three of them lay perfectly still, staring up at the ceiling.

"I do not know. But we cannot stay here in England."

The Palmer girls spent the whole of that first day in Elsie's room. Cecile brought them trays of food and pots of tea—all of which sat untouched.

At midday on the second day, she urged them to change into their normal clothes and join her for lunch. They did so, reluctantly, and returned to Elsie's room immediately after.

That evening, though, Cecile could hear the girls talking together in the room. She felt very sad for them. So many mothers died in childbirth, and their daughters never knew their love. She did not know which was worse.

On the third day, Cecile entered the breakfast room and was surprised to find all three Palmer girls bathed, dressed, and seated at the table. They ate in silence, but she knew it was a vast improvement.

She looked around at them and marveled at just how similar they all appeared. Queen's doe eyes and curly hair had found their way into each of her daughters, though in different manifestations.

Dorothy, quite the young woman, had just turned 14. She had the same porcelain-doll look as her older sister—bright, flawless skin and perfectly straight teeth.

Marjory, though only 13 years old, had the true look of a high-bred Englishwoman, with a pert noise and fashionable hair. Tall and thin, she looked the most like their father of any of them—a fact she knew Elsie envied.

"Elsie," Dorothy broke the silence. "When does Father come?"

"I hardly know," she replied. "In a week, perhaps two."

Marjory bowed her head and began to cry softly. Elsie rose from her place at the table and embraced her.

"There, there," she whispered. "Everything will be fine."

"You do not know that!" Dorothy nearly shouted at her. "You have no idea whether everything will be fine."

"Of course I do not, Dos, but we must be brave. For Father's sake."

"You act like it is going to be a happy reunion with Father and the servants and the townspeople," she snapped, "but I do not remember Glen Eyrie, and what is more ... I do not care!"

Elsie looked for a moment as though she had been slapped across the face. She dearly loved their home in Colorado, but she knew her sisters had no memories of the place.

Dorothy, however, felt trapped. No matter where she had been born, she was an Englishwoman now. Father had written to her for years, with stories of railroad wars and Indian fights, outbreaks of tuberculosis and devastating fires. How would she survive in the West?

"Do you remember what Father sent me for my birthday last year?" Dorothy continued. "A doll. A doll! As if I were five years old. I will always be a little girl to him, and I cannot bear the thought."

Marjory pursed her lips and Elsie replied, "Surely you do not mean that." Outbursts of this nature were all too common with Dorothy, but Elsie thought she was particularly out of control. "Well, it does not matter much now. We do not belong here anymore," she snapped. "We belong with Father. We cannot stay."

Dorothy folded her arms in front of her chest and quickly left the room. She needed air.

"DO NOT TEASE ME, Leo," Elsie said to the young man leaning against the wall. They were alone in the dining room; her sisters had retired early to bed that evening. He stared at her intently, with the handsomest eyes Elsie had ever seen.

"I am not, I promise," he said and touched her face.

"You and I both know you will never come visit me in Colorado," Elsie replied and pulled back gently. Leo came in closer and kissed her lips.

"Leopold Hamilton Myers!" Elsie cried and peered around to make sure no one was watching. "I cannot believe you just did that!"

"Oh, what, kiss you?" he replied. "You wanted me to."

Elsie blushed deeply. "I did not."

"You have wanted me to kiss you since the first time we danced together, admit it." He said and reached out to tuck a curl behind her ear.

Elsie did not answer for a moment. "You are the most impertinent man I have ever met," she said and turned to leave.

"Wait a moment!" Leo called. "Please do not go." Elsie turned to look at him. "I am sorry I am being such an ass."

Elsie studied her hands and dared not look at him as he confessed. "The truth is, I am going to miss you very much."

She looked up at him then and smiled. "And I you. Very much."

"Can we start over?" he asked as he motioned for her to sit down. They sat together in silence for a few minutes, listening to the servants bustling about outside the door.

"I can still remember that dance perfectly," she began. "I wore my favorite blue muslin gown, do you remember, with the silver beads. You had come with the Mastersons, and I fairly begged Maria Masterson to introduce us. She did, and we danced that first waltz together.

"I was so nervous I thought my heart would beat out of my chest. But you, you were confident. You smiled at me and said something funny to make me laugh. I knew after that we would be the best of friends."

Leo smiled sadly at this recollection. "I was nervous, too."

"You never were," she said and looked down.

"I was, too," he replied. "You looked so lovely. And you were so young."

"I was fifteen," she said. "Golly, that was a long time ago."

A knock at the door brought them back to the present. A footman entered, carrying a tray, to remove the dishes.

"Our apologies," Elsie said and stood up. "Mister Myers was just leaving."

Elsie and Leo walked together to the front hallway, where the butler helped him into his overcoat. He turned to her and kissed her hand gently.

"Write to me?" she asked.

"I promise," he said and stepped into his carriage.

Elsie frowned as she watched it pulled away.

IT HAD BEEN 10 days since Mama's passing, and the girls still had no sign of Father. *Did his ship sink in the middle of the Atlantic? Had he been delayed somehow at the port in Southampton?* Elsie sat pondering these thoughts when she heard Mr. Brown, the butler, pull open the big oak doors that graced the front of Loseley Park and spied a man climbing out of a hired carriage.

Her heart began to beat faster and faster. *What is wrong with you?* she asked herself. *It is only—*

"Father!" Marjory squealed and ran across the hall and straight into his arms. A thin man with a bushy mustache and warm eyes stared back at them. He cut a fine figure, and his eyes conveyed strength and gentleness. Father was already many years into middle age, but he still walked with a determined and purposeful gait.

"My darling," he said, sadly. "I have missed you so." He set her down and stroked her cheek warmly, then he hugged her again in a rib-crushing embrace. He let go when he caught sight of the other girls making their way to him. Elsie ran to him and jumped into his arms, just as Marjory had done. Dorothy, however, hung back, hesitant.

"Is that my little Dos? Heavens all." Father pulled her into a hug, her arms stiff by her sides. He pulled back and studied her face. "You look so very like your mother."

Dorothy did not respond but smiled modestly at him. *Did he bring a miniature tea set with him? Or maybe a stuffed bear?* she thought but then felt very guilty. *Dos,* she told herself, *you must not be so heartless. Father is a good man. Get a hold of yourself.*

The butler took Father's overcoat and hat then spoke briefly with the valet and ordered a bath to be drawn for him before dinner.

"Thank you, Ainsley," Father said to the valet. "I know I will feel better after I wash the road off of me."

Elsie grabbed hold of Father's arm and led him to a chair, as the other girls surrounded him. "I have something for you, Father," she said.

She brought out a small box she had stowed away in a pocket. She opened it and pressed a small ring into the middle of Father's wide hand. He looked closely at it and rubbed his fingers over the engraving: "WJP to Queen, November 8, 1870."

"Oh, Queen," he moaned softly and pressed his lips to the ring, tears streaming down his face. "I am so sorry, my love."

Elsie had always considered Father a passionate man, but she had rarely seen him cry. She could only recall one other time: the day they had set sail for England. She imagined he had probably cried on his wedding day and on each of his daughter's birth days, but she would add today to the very short list.

Elsie squeezed his shoulder. "Father, she knew you were on your way here, but you had to come so far—"

"I should have been here with her. I shall never forgive myself for that," he cried. His daughters crowded around him then, and the four of them embraced.

THE MORNING OF THEIR departure to America dawned bright and beautiful, a rare sight for England that time of year. Cecile hurried about the room, packing last-minute items into a large trunk. Elsie had already dressed and eaten breakfast downstairs, but she let the other girls sleep in just a little longer than normal. Today was the big day. She could not contain her excitement.

Over the last several weeks, Father wrapped up Mama's affairs—finding tenants for Loseley Park, closing out her bank account, and paying calls to all of their friends and relatives. Queen was beloved by people far and wide, so this last part took some time, but it made Father and the girls happy to know Queen would be missed by so many.

Elsie wandered the halls of the grand estate, thinking about Mama and wondering what changes she would find back home. Heartbroken is not a strong enough word to describe how Elsie felt to leave Colorado all those years ago. Every day since their arrival in gloomy England, she had tried to recall the sights and sounds of the little pioneer town, and to remember the names and faces of those she had left behind.

Her life in England had been happy. She eventually made new friends—Leo and Caroline, in particular—and traveled all around Europe. But she always knew she belonged in Colorado.

The year she had turned 17, Father came on his yearly visit and took Elsie on a special trip to Switzerland, just the two of them. They shared a deep love of the mountains, and the magnificent Alps were the perfect place for a pair such as them. She had always adored Father, but on that trip they became something more than father and daughter; they became friends.

So much so that a year ago Elsie convinced Mama to allow her to travel back home to Colorado by herself—with Cecile as a chaperone, of course. She and Father spent a glorious few months exploring the Rockies, dining at Father's hotel with her friends, and roaming the grounds of Glen Eyrie.

Glen Eyrie, how I long to see you again, she thought.

Father and Mama's fascination with old European architecture inspired them to create the most magnificent house west of the

Mississippi—to Elsie, at least. Father had made many improvements to the house over the years, and Elsie understood he had many more in mind.

She could not wait to look out over the expansive grounds and see big horn sheep and bald eagles and perhaps a squaw or two. Father had written to tell her the Indians no longer set up summer camp in that valley, but perhaps they would make a special appearance just for her.

It had been her, after all, that had fascinated the squaws in the first place. When Elsie was but a wee baby, Mama was busy bathing her in the nursery when she heard footsteps out in the hallway. Mama's stepmother, Ellen, was there with baby Maud, and the pair were chatting and laughing together as they washed and diapered their babies.

Baby Maud saw the visitors first and reached out to them from the washbasin with her chubby fingers. As the women turned, they saw in the doorway to the nursery a Ute Indian squaw with her husband, whose name Mama always said was Happy Jack or something of the sort. Fascinated by the white people, the Indians often peered through the windows and even entered the house unannounced.

They spoke in broken English, which pleased Mama immensely, and asked the white women if they would bathe their baby, as well. Mama happily obliged, and the squaw unwrapped a tiny infant from the papoose on her back. Ellen was beside herself as the squaw and her husband approached, but Mama, unafraid, eagerly studied the expertly beaded and intricate leatherwork of the papoose.

"This is lovely," she said to the squaw, who only nodded and smiled.

She placed her baby in Mama's arms and observed closely as Ellen and Mama bathed and powdered the infant. They dressed the baby in a white cotton gown, and the Indians thanked them. Then they left the room and walked out the front door. When they were gone, Ellen let out a loud breath, and Mama belly laughed for a solid five minutes.

At first Mama swore Ellen to secrecy, knowing Father would not be pleased and might decide to have a word with the Indian chief. But years later, they told Father the tale, and they all had a good laugh about it.

Mama had been very sad to hear the Utes did not return, but she knew in her heart it was no longer safe for them to stay.

Elsie heard her sisters' voices in the corridor. She stepped into the hall to see Dorothy and Marjory descend the carved wooden staircase to the breakfast room below.

"There you girls are," she said. "I was just about to send a search party upstairs. Cook prepared a delicious going-away breakfast for us. Eat quickly, the carriage will be here within the hour. Chop chop!" she called gaily, to her sisters' surprise.

Dorothy resisted the urge to roll her eyes. "I do not know how she can be so cheerful about this," she confided to Marjory as Elsie hurried ahead into the breakfast room. "Our departure is not a cause for celebration."

"Cheer up, dearest," Marjory responded. "She does not mean anything by it."

After breakfast, Father and the girls meticulously searched each room to make certain the servants had packed everything. Most of their belongings had been sent ahead of them to America, but a few trunks remained behind to accompany them on their long voyage across the sea.

"They packed your portrait, then?" Father asked Elsie.

Before she could reply, Dorothy cut in and with a teasing voice said, "Oooooh, your portrait. Oooooh, Mister Sargent."

Elsie shot her an icy glare and said, "Yes, Father, that was the first thing I had them pack. I stood over them as they did so and urged the maids to use extra care. A John Singer Sargent might be worth a fortune one day."

"I would count on it, darling," Father said with assurance.

Confident they had not left anything behind, the Palmers and Cecile donned coats, hats, and gloves and prepared for the journey to the coast. The servants of Loseley Park stood lined up outside the grand oak doors, waiting to wish them farewell and safe voyage. The girls took turns hugging the women servants and shaking hands with the men servants. Everything was about to change for them, too. The new tenants would arrive the following day.

They loaded into the carriage, their trunks perched precariously atop. As they pulled away from the stately mansion, Dorothy turned in her seat to look back at the house and the servants waving. "One day I will see you again," she said quietly to herself. "I hope."

Chapter Two

A man must go to the mountains for health, but also to get a true
insight into things.

GENERAL WILLIAM JACKSON PALMER

EARLY SPRING 1895

"ARE WE NEARLY THERE?" Dorothy moaned.

"I am afraid we still have many miles to go, darling," Palmer
responded.

I wish he would not call me that, Dorothy thought. *Darling. As if I were
still four years old.*

They bounced and jiggled from Surrey to Southampton on the
southern coast, a journey of nearly 60 miles. They stopped overnight
along the way in Medstead and lodged at the local pub. That decision
ended up being a bad one. The beds were creaky, the food was
unsatisfactory, and the gentlemen lodgers were no gentlemen at all.

After what felt like days, they finally arrived in the bustling port town. Dorothy and Marjory gazed in awe upon the ships that were nearly 4 times the size of Loseley Park and 10 times taller. They felt frightened at the thought of a whole week at sea. They had traveled abroad, of course, to visit France, but the English Channel is a mere fraction of the distance they embarked on now.

They boarded the massive ship and quickly found their new "homes" in First Class. The furnishings in their state rooms were more than satisfactory, which Elsie noted with delight. The girls preferred to spend their days sleeping in, lounging about the upper decks, and playing games with other young ladies. Father did boring things, in his daughters' opinions—like playing cards with the First Class men and talking business in the Men's Lounge—but it made him exceedingly happy.

Leo ... Elsie wrote on a sheet of stationery. *I miss you* ...

She crumpled up the note and began again. *Leo, how are you?*

"No," she said to herself and tossed the second note in the bin.

"What are you doing?" Marjory asked as she entered their state room.

Elsie looked up at her and sighed. "Just writing to Leo. But I do not know what to say."

"Why do you hesitate?"

"I do not know, really."

Marjory pondered this for a moment. "Perhaps simply tell him you miss him."

"I cannot do that," Elsie said. She *did* miss him, but she could not bear the thought of Leo reading those words.

Marjory squeezed her sister's hand and left the room.

AFTER SEVEN DAYS AT sea, their ship finally arrived in New York.

"Look!" Marjory shouted to her sisters as they crowded around the deck. "I can see Lady Liberty!"

"Do not call it that," Dorothy snapped. "You sound like a foreigner."

Marjory and Cecile looked at each other and laughed. "We *are* foreigners, or do not you remember?" Marjory replied.

"Yes, of course, but we are Americans, too."

Dorothy and Marjory were too young to remember their first trip to New York City. This time, everything was bright and new. They marveled at the blue skies over a city so large—so unlike London. They pointed at the skyscrapers and extension bridges connecting Manhattan to Brooklyn and beyond. It was unlike anything they had ever seen. New York City was a town ahead of its time, and it thrilled them. They wished Father would forget about Colorado and allow them to live here instead, but, alas, he would not be convinced.

They lodged for the night at the new Waldorf Hotel on 5th Avenue. Father told them most New Yorkers hated the hotel, but he adored it, and so did the girls. It was both lavish and modern, in a great location near the best shops, and close to Central Park. What could be better, they thought.

The following morning, a hired carriage transported them to Grand Central Station, where they boarded a train to Kansas City.

"Is this one of yours, Father?" Marjory asked him, referring to the train.

"No, darling," he replied, "but we will board one of mine later, when we get to Kansas."

As Father turned away, Dorothy rolled her eyes, and Marjory elbowed her.

The journey to Kansas City took three nights and four days, across foothills and streams, the most expansive river they had ever seen (even bigger than the Thames!), and endless miles of open prairie. Marjory secretly hoped to see Indians riding horses, shooting arrows at buffalo—just as she imagined the Wild West—but she had to settle for antelope and the occasional deer.

When they reached Kansas, they did not bother to lodge for the night but boarded the next train—one of Father's—almost immediately. Once they were settled in to their private compartment, Father left to speak with the conductor; he did so several times throughout the trip. Elsie supposed he missed his old life on the open rails and wanted to reminisce.

"Oooh, this is so exciting!" Elsie squealed, patting Dorothy's leg. "Father helped build this railway, you know."

"Yes, of course I know," Dorothy mumbled.

"Cheer up, Dos, Father does not deserve to see you with such a long face," Marjory pleaded with her. "Especially since he has been so dear to arrange our travel and make sure we have our creature comforts. See here," she said, spreading her arms wide, "we are in First Class, headed to our new home, surrounded by the most beautiful countryside we have ever seen."

"Hmphf," Dorothy said and sat back against the padded seat, arms folded.

"Oh, do not be so bad-tempered," Elsie said.

"IS THIS NOT A lovely station?" Elsie remarked to her sisters as they arrived in Denver's Union Station.

"It is, indeed," Marjory replied.

"Father, how much further?" Dorothy asked.

"We are nearly there," he said and glanced at her. "It should take a little over two hours to reach town."

At Union Station, they boarded their third and final train: a black narrow gauge engine from the Denver & Rio Grande Western Railroad, Father's brainchild and proudest achievement.

Leaving Denver, they chugged south, rising in elevation over 2,000 feet, up and over several foothills, and through a wide, low valley dotted with cattle and a small farmhouse.

"What a bizarre landscape," Marjory remarked as they passed flat-top foothills covered in scrub oak.

"Is that a castle?" Dorothy remarked as she pointed to a large rock formation at the top of one of the foothills.

"My, it does look like one," Marjory added.

Father only smiled and Elsie chuckled.

"What?" Dorothy asked. "What did I say?"

Elsie looked at Father and replied, "This town is called Castle Rock."

"See?" Dorothy said. "I must not be the only one who thinks it looks like a castle."

As they continued south towards Colorado Springs, they crested the tallest foothill yet and descended into town. The majestic Pike's Peak came into full view, presiding over the town like a mother over her beloved child.

"Now *this* I hope you remember, girls," Father said eagerly, motioning to the peak.

Dorothy and Marjory peered out the train window at the famous peak, the summit completely covered in snow. Mama and Elsie had talked about the peak many times. They said it was breathtakingly beautiful and that it rose up over the town below, as if with outstretched arms. But they did not remember it from their childhood.

"Only from the photographs you sent, I am afraid, Father," Marjory replied.

Father looked sad but only briefly before he said, "Never mind. You are here now, and that is what matters."

Dorothy and Marjory were amazed at what the fledgling pioneer town had become in their absence. Mama had always described it as full of dusty roads and white tents, but these had given way to long, leafy boulevards and stately homes. Colorado Springs was certainly no little town anymore. Even Elsie was struck by the changes. It seemed to have grown double its size in the year since she had last been there.

"We have arrived," Father said as they chugged into the Denver and Rio Grande Depot.

All three girls looked out the window then and caught sight of a large group of people. One person held up a sign made from what looked like an old bed sheet.

"Welcome home!" Marjory read. "Father, is this for us?"

"Yes, I believe it is." He blushed.

The crowd cheered as the Palmer family disembarked onto the wooden platform. Elsie recognized several of the faces in the crowd and waved at them. The crowd circled around them as Father attempted to introduce his girls to each of them.

Then, Father led them inside the station to speak to the porter in charge of collecting their baggage. Father's coachman sat waiting for them on the street and loaded their bags onto the carriage. Father mounted his favorite horse, The Moor—an enormous black creature— and the girls climbed in. One more wave to the crowd, and they pulled away from the station.

They rode home, a distance of over 10 miles, in animated discussion about the beautiful views around them. They traveled up and over several bluffs, taking turns sticking their heads out of the carriage window to survey the mountains that stretched across the horizon and far up into the sky. They marveled at the picturesque peaks and vowed to visit every inch of them. Occasionally, Father poked his head inside the carriage door to point out a house, or ridge, or scenic view Mama had particularly loved.

As they entered the Valley of the Eagle's Nest, as Glen Eyrie was called, Dorothy was struck by a sudden memory. The winding path and iron gate before her seemed so familiar. She closed her eyes for a moment to attempt to recall the memory. She could see little girls dressed in white pinafores, frolicking and laughing.

Dorothy knocked on the roof of the carriage to signal the coachman to halt. Father rode up beside them and dismounted.

"Did we use to play here?" Dorothy asked Father.

His eyes lit up as Elsie responded, "We used to sit out here with Nanny Tante and give cups of water to visitors. What a funny thing to remember."

"I do remember it, though," she said and sat back against her seat.

She closed her eyes again. The name "Nanny Tante" had awakened more memories, and she smiled to herself as she thought of the three of them as little girls, handing water cups to strangers.

As they followed the tree-lined path, they crossed over two low stone bridges and curved past a wide, sweeping lawn. Massive red, spiked rocks jutted straight up from the earth, and Elsie pointed them out to her sisters as they went by.

"That one's Major Domo. And over there, that tall one is King Arthur's Seat."

The names sounded absolutely bizarre and foreign to Dorothy, like descriptions of another world. She liked it, but part of her wondered if she would ever grow accustomed to this strange place.

Elsie could read the expression on her sister's face and said, "Odd names, I know. Mama and her siblings named them."

As they rounded the last bend and Glen Eyrie came into full view, Father became very excited.

"Oh, Father," Marjory said, "it is so beautiful."

Even Dorothy approved of the sight before them. She nodded her head as she took it all in. Glen Eyrie was perfectly situated amid jagged cliffs, enormous pine trees, and the unusual red, spiked rocks.

"Welcome home, at last," Father said and smiled broadly. He had been waiting for this moment for over 10 years, and it could not be more perfect. Except, of course, that Queen was not with them.

Father led them to the carriage house—a two-story, wooden structure with several stables and rooms above for the grooms. He introduced the girls to Jesse Bass, the young and handsome head groom who tenderly cared for Father's prize horses. Out of the corner of her eye, Dorothy spotted two footmen who seemed to appear out of nowhere from behind a green door cut into the hillside. The door guarded the entrance to what looked like a tunnel beneath the ground. Before she could see where it led, the servants picked up their trunks and disappeared into the darkness.

"Do you require the horses any longer, Sir?" Jesse asked.

"No, thank you. We will continue on foot to the house."

Father led the girls out of the carriage house courtyard and around to the front of the house to take in the full view. Marjory and Dorothy's eyes were round as they surveyed their new home.

"Magnificent, no?" Elsie asked them. "Father has done so much to it."

It is like something from a storybook, Marjory thought.

A magnificent, three-story, Tudor Revival-style house loomed over them, blocking out the sun and casting a large shadow across the wide lawn. It appeared nearly as large as Loseley Park, though not nearly as old. It had leaded glass windows, gables, arched doorways, a large tower, and 22 rooms of absolute splendor—a real work of art.

Dorothy's eyes traveled up and up to the round tower room at the very top. Father noticed her gazing at the tower and said, "That was Mama's favorite spot. She used to spend hours painting in there. You can see for miles."

Dorothy found it odd to think of regal Mama living in such a wild and uncultured place, but she must have been happy, for she had been deeply saddened when she had to leave.

But perhaps she was sad to leave Father, she thought, *and not this valley.*

Her thoughts were interrupted then by the sound of a large animal running towards them.

"What is that—!"

"Yorick!" Father shouted as an enormous dog bounded towards him and tried to leap into his arms. The girls watched as Father chased the dog around the lawn a bit and scratched its belly as it rolled over.

"Yorick, Yorick," Marjory repeated to herself. "Why does that name sound so familiar?"

"Ha ha!" Dorothy laughed as it dawned on her. "Father, did you really name that dog after *Hamlet*?"

"You bet I did! I knew you would appreciate that," Father said and winked at her.

"It took me months to get it, Dos, so you are way ahead of me," Elsie said.

"Oh dear, I am afraid I do not get it at all," Marjory replied.

"The dog is a Great Dane. *Hamlet*. Yorick?"

Marjory just shook her head as Elsie whispered in her ear, "I will tell you later."

The enormous front door opened behind them, and a dark-haired Italian man ran out to greet them.

"Welcome! Welcome!" he exclaimed.

Calixte Bertolotti—Berty, as he was affectionately called—Father's butler and valet, had emigrated to America some 20 years before. Back home in Turin, Italy, he had trained as a footman and then as an under butler. He had a proclivity for foreign languages and spoke several—with no trace of his native accent.

When he had first arrived at Glen Eyrie, he had fallen instantly in love with the beautiful, young English cook. Father always said the love affair had awakened something in Berty—something akin to a long-hid comedian, lurking just outside the edges of Berty's personality. In fact, when he fell head over heels for the cook, he woke up the next day with an arsenal of silly jokes. He and his bride, and their two daughters, lived in a cottage near the gate house.

Berty led them inside the house, where the housekeeper waited to greet them. "My, my, my, you have grown so much!" she exclaimed as Dorothy and Marjory stepped forward. "You were but *wee bairns* last time I saw you," she said and scooped them both up into a hug.

Mrs. Simmons was a voluptuous Scottish woman of advanced age, who presided over Glen Eyrie with all the nurturing of a grandmama and the ferocity of a mother wolf. She was jolly and caring and loved the Palmer family as her own, but she took her job very seriously. One time, when Elsie was younger, Berty had spilled the beans about the terrible misfortune of Mrs. Simmons' given name. "Persimmon Simmons," Berty had said and slapped his knee. "What a name!"

"My mother gave me that name," Mrs. Simmons had shot back. "The woman loved her garden. I have one sister named Parsnip and another named Daffodil. My brother, Seamus, is the only one of us who came out unscathed."

At Loseley Park, they had scores of house servants—over 30 in all—and each girl had a personal maid. Here at Glen Eyrie, however, things were very different. Father employed fewer than eight house servants, and he considered all of them personal friends. He knew not only their family members' names but also a bit about their hopes and dreams for the future, and, in any way he could, he helped them realize those dreams. Father was special that way. He did not see status or rank—or at least took very little notice of it. To him, the men and women he employed deserved dignity and respect just like any other person.

"Shall we pass through?" Mrs. Simmons said and motioned to the large, wooden door.

IN THE SERVANTS' HALLWAY, two sisters huddled together as they whispered. They watched from a third-story window as the Palmers arrived and marveled at the girls' fine clothing and fashionable hairstyles.

"I wonder what they will be like," the younger sister, Lanora, said.

"I hardly know," Anna replied. "Their father is a kind man. We can only hope they are, too."

Palmer had hired Anna and Lanora Knight not six months previously. He knew his girls would be accustomed to having maids to tend to their needs, and he wanted to do everything in his power to make their transition as smooth as possible. The two housemaids came highly recommended by his dear friend Dr. Bell; he had three of their brothers in his employ.

Lanora had much to learn, but Anna was a natural. She had been a housemaid in a large manor and knew her way around curling irons and muslin gowns. For now, Lanora would tidy rooms and pick up after the other servants. But Father and Mrs. Simmons had big plans for the young girl.

DOWNSTAIRS, MRS. SIMMONS LED the girls to Elsie's quarters, a lovely, round room on the second floor with windows on three sides that overlooked the grassy lawn below. It was situated next door to Mama's old sitting room. Father had let her choose the room during her trip to Colorado last year. She wanted to be close to Mama's favorite spaces.

Elsie saw the footmen had already brought her trunk up; it was waiting for her on the bed. As the others continued on, she remained behind to remove her hat and coat. The largest windows faced east, which provided good light in the morning hours. That was when Elsie most enjoyed reading, in the morning before her sisters had awoken. Her mind relished in the solitude and the freedom to explore books without fear of being interrupted. Sometimes she would lose hours of the day, lost in her own head. Often, she would read to disguise her daydreaming, but her sisters could always tell when she had been transported to another place—she would forget to keep turning the pages.

Every time Father had visited them in England, he had brought Elsie a new book bound in rich-smelling leather. It was their shared joy. The books were always Classics—Milton and Wordsworth, Dickens and Yeats. Father also worshiped the Romantic poets; he could recite John Keats's *Endymion* by heart. Dorothy, too, was a reader, but of vastly different subjects, such as astronomy and science.

Sometimes, Father went against his better judgment and brought Elsie a "silly" book or two to enjoy, usually a mystery novel or a poem collection by Emily Dickinson. Elsie admired that most about Father— pleasure was never off-limits to him. He was the most righteous man she knew, but he never failed to enjoy himself and to allow others to pursue joy, as well. These "silly" books always felt like a luxury, an escape when her thoughts became too melancholy.

Elsie walked over to the fireplace and crouched down to rub her fingers along the hearth. *If only a servant saw me like this!* she thought. Under her fingers she could feel the rough edges of stones and shells, remnants of a time gone by. She had placed the treasures there herself many years ago, with the help of her playmate, Aunt Maud. When

Mama had come to Colorado after her wedding, her father, stepmother, and six younger sisters and brothers had come, too.

Elsie and Maud had lived there together as girls and referred to each other as such, but as Elsie grew, her grandmother insisted she call her playmate "Aunt Maud." It always felt strange, though, for she was not even a year older.

I should ask Father for a small allowance to redecorate this room, she thought to herself as she surveyed the unfashionable bedding and window dressings. She would have a fresh start, and so would they.

Down the hallway, the party came to Dorothy's room. It was somewhat smaller but beautifully furnished, with a mahogany desk and a lovely fireplace in one corner. A fire crackled merrily in the hearth.

"And this way to Miss Marjory's room," Mrs. Simmons said and guided them a little further down the hallway.

They peeked into the room and saw the mirror image of Dorothy's, right down to a similar desk and merry fireplace.

"I'll leave you to settle in and prepare for supper, then," Mrs. Simmons said and gently closed Marjory's door behind her.

Dorothy settled in to her new quarters and bathed quickly before slipping into a fresh gown from her trunk. When she felt presentable enough, she stepped into the hallway in search of her sisters. She rapped lightly on Marjory's door. Her sister opened it, and Dorothy saw that she, too, had bathed and changed gowns.

"You look very refreshed, Dos," she said. "Feeling better?"

"A little," she replied. "Can I tell you something?"

"Of course."

Dorothy paused for a moment and looked down at her feet. Then, in a small voice, she said, "I am scared."

Marjory went to her sister and wrapped her arms around her waist. "As am I," she said. "Very much so. I do not know how we will grow accustomed to this new place, but we must try. We must make the most of it."

Dorothy let out a large breath. "I promise to try."

"Good." Marjory smiled. "Come on, let us find Elsie."

They found their sister downstairs with Father in the sitting room. The pair were chatting animatedly, and Father looked up as they came in.

"Ah, there you are," Father said. "Just in time."

Father had ordered a simple spread of cold cut meats and cheeses and some soft bread. The girls were accustomed to having a glass of wine with supper, even the younger girls, but Father did not allow alcohol of any kind. In fact, he did not allow alcohol to be served in any of the establishments in Colorado Springs. He said liquor stole away a person's best asset: their mind. And the girls knew all too well that Father prized a person's mind above all else. Elsie knew better than to mention it to Father and prayed her sisters wouldn't either.

After supper, they gathered around the fireplace and listened while Father read a few passages from a worn Bible. Mama had tried to preserve the traditions of Father's faith, but—admittedly—they often skipped the evening Bible readings. As the girls would soon find out, skipping it was not an option for Father.

Dorothy and Marjory retired to their rooms early, exhausted from the long voyage, but Elsie stayed behind for a moment. There was something she wanted to ask Father.

"Father," she said, "would you mind if I squirreled away one of your Dickens? Perhaps *Dombey and Son*? Mine are all packed up."

"I have an even better idea," he said and led her down a corridor adjoining the dining room. They entered Father's den, which had low bookcases encircling the room, with a large stone fireplace in one corner and two wingback chairs. A large American flag, several rifles, and a shadow box containing Father's medals from the war lined the walls. It felt cozy. She ran her fingers over the spines of his extensive book collection, tracing the names of authors she knew so well they felt like old friends.

"Most of my books I keep out in the library, but these are my personal favorites," he said and pulled out a small, leather-bound book from one of the shelves. He handed it to her and said, "Read this one. You will like it."

"*Ramona*," she read the spine.

"Helen Hunt Jackson," he said. "She was a local."

"Indeed?" Elsie remarked, pleasantly surprised at the thought of a famous author who had lived close by.

AT DAYBREAK THE NEXT morning, Elsie found herself gravitating towards the sitting chair in the corner of her room. She folded her legs under her and snuggled down deep into the cushions. She reached for the window latch and swung it wide open so she could hear the birds chirping in the trees. She opened the first pages of *Ramona* and began to read.

After nearly an hour, she heard movement in Dorothy's room next door. She reluctantly set the book aside. She knew the others would be awake soon and rang the bell for the maid. A half hour later, she was dressed and prepared for the day.

At Loseley Park, they had a French maid who had made it her job to master the latest fashionable hairstyles. This maid, Anna, possessed no such skill, but Elsie imagined her need for such finery was firmly in the past. Regardless, one maid to assist three girls would be quite the chore. She made a mental note to ask Father to hire at least one more. Maybe she could convince him to hire a French maid. More outlandish things have happened!

Exiting her room, she found her sisters at the top of the stairs.

"We were just about to go down," Marjory said.

Elsie walked with them down to the main floor. The sound of clinking dishes reached their ears, and Father's strong voice emanated from a nearby room. As they entered, Dorothy was surprised to find that the room made almost a complete circle.

This must be the first floor of the tower, she noted to herself.

The breakfast room was empty except for a footman and Father, who greeted them with his usual smile and wide-open arms.

"Good morning, darlings," he said. "Are you well-rested? Please, sit.

Cook made us quite the breakfast this morning."

Elsie glanced at the sideboard, which was filled to capacity with silver platters of sausages, eggs, pancakes, and a mysterious teapot full of what she dearly hoped was plain, black tea.

As they tucked in to their breakfasts, the footman offered Elsie the contents of the teapot. He began to pour, and for a moment Elsie half-expected to see coffee come pouring out of the pot; it was, after all, Father's favorite morning treat. Instead, her cup began to fill with rich, dark, black tea that smelled faintly of vanilla. She tipped her cup slightly to show Marjory, who was seated next to her.

"Tea, Father?" Marjory said with a tone of surprise. "Did you order tea?"

"I cannot expect my girls to abandon all of their favorite comforts," he replied. "Even though tea seems a weak substitute for coffee."

"We are English, after all. I expect we will take tea three times a day just like we always do," Dorothy replied curtly. "I will never grow accustomed to ... coffee," she said as she scrunched up her nose.

Her words stung Father, but he just laughed politely and turned the conversation to the house. "I have many improvements in mind, and I covet your help," he said and looked round at his girls. "You managed to turn stuffy, cold Loseley Park into a homey place. I trust you will do the same for Glen Eyrie."

"Father, I cannot imagine how we could improve upon the house, truly," Marjory replied. "It is stunning as it is."

He reached across the table to stroke her cheek affectionately. "Perhaps. But your mama had big plans for this house. I would love nothing more than to turn those plans into reality."

ELSIE WAS SURPRISED BY the amount of visitors Father entertained throughout the course of a day—even more than he did a year ago. First, it was his solicitor, then his business partners, then a friend from the club, and finally his physician. Elsie recognized this last one almost instantly.

"Can it be Doctor Jameson?!" she squealed as she ran towards him.

A portly man of 75 years with a white beard and a *pince nez* stretched out his arms and crouched a bit to allow Elsie to embrace him. "Well, well, well! Only a year has passed and yet, here you are, a proper lady."

"I have missed you," Elsie said and smiled affectionately at him. When she was a small child, she loved Dr. Jameson second only to Father. He had known her since she was a small baby, and she looked up to him as a granddaughter would to a beloved grandfather.

"Wait right here," she said. "I must fetch my sisters. You will not believe how much *they* have grown."

Moments later, the three Palmer girls surrounded Dr. Jameson as he marveled at their much-altered appearances. "It has been a lifetime," he said. "I suppose you do not remember me."

"I do," Marjory said shyly. "At least I think I do. I remember your eyes. They are very kind."

"How marvelous!" the doctor replied and clasped her hands. "My, how you look like your mother."

"Everyone says so. But I think all three of us resemble her in our own ways. Elsie has her eyes; Dos, her hair; and I have her ivory skin."

"Indeed. You are quite right."

Berty cleared his throat loudly. He was standing in the hallway, waiting to bring the doctor to Father's den.

Elsie turned around at the noise to see Berty with a mock-stern face. "Pardon us, Berty," Elsie said and laughed, "we got caught up. You came to see Father," she turned to Dr. Jameson. "Please, do not let us keep you from your business."

Dr. Jameson tipped his hat at her, smiled at the other two girls, and followed Berty to the den.

When they had left, Marjory asked, "Why is Father seeing his physician? Is he sick?

"No, indeed," Elsie said. "Father is as healthy as a horse. No, he must be here on other business."

Marjory was not convinced but shook her head in agreement. "Well,

I will return to my room. I was nearly finished unpacking."

She reached the second-floor landing and paused in front of her door; she could hear someone humming just inside. She reached for the door handle and swung it open to reveal a tall, slender girl in a starched, white uniform wearing a cap with streamers flowing down her back. She twirled and danced as she held up Marjory's finest gown.

"Why, hello," Marjory said to her.

"Oh!" the girl exclaimed and spun around. "I do apologize—" She quickly laid the gown on the bed.

Marjory extended her hand to her and said, "My name is Marjory— what is yours?"

"Lanora, miss," the young girl said and bowed slightly, coloring. She pressed her hand against her cheek. "Lanora Knight. I am just a hall girl right now, but one day I know I can be head housemaid," the girl said rapidly.

"A hall girl?" Marjory asked, unfamiliar with the term.

"Yes, miss. I wait on Cook and Berty and Missus Simmons. But sometimes they have me make beds and light fires, miss, when the housemaid needs help. That's my sister, the housemaid. Her name is Anna."

"I see. In England we would call that a *tweeny*, a between maid. Very nice to make your acquaintance, Lanora. Please, call me Marjory. How old are you?"

"Fourteen."

"I will be fourteen in a few months," Marjory said.

"Then we will be the same age!" Lanora said in delight. "Can I call you Miss Marjory?"

Marjory smiled politely and said, "Of course. How long have you worked for my father?"

"I have only been here six months, Miss Marjory."

"Indeed." Marjory replied. "And how do you like it?"

"Master Palmer is a very kind man. He is kinder to me than my own pa ever was. See, my mother had nine of us children. Three of our brothers live in Manitou Springs, but our parents and other siblings live in the mountains, in a small place called Crested Butte. My pa used to dig for gold, but they have been scraping by for several years. My ma wanted me and Anna to have a better shot at life, so she sent us here."

Marjory felt saddened by Lanora's story, but she knew it was common among the working class to leave one's family at a young age in order to find work. Marjory had never known the sting of poverty, but in a way she could relate to Lanora's plight; she had had to leave her home—and loved ones—twice in her short life.

"It must be wonderful to work in the same house as your sister," Marjory said. "I have two older sisters—you may have met them?"

"Yes, Miss Marjory, I laid fires for them in their rooms this morning."

Marjory only nodded. "Did you never attend school, Lanora?"

"I used to go to school, but my parents needed me to produce wages. My sister and me, we send every penny home. Well almost, anyway," she said and blushed slightly. "Sometimes I keep a penny or two from my wages. I am saving up to buy us tickets home for a couple of days this summer. Crested Butte is cut off from the world during the winter months, but in the summer you can travel by train most of the way and then by rented carriage up the winding valley. It is very beautiful there in summer. Even more beautiful than here, Miss Marjory, if you can believe it. The hills are filled with wildflowers, every color, as far as the eye can see."

"I cannot imagine anything more beautiful than that," Marjory said genuinely.

Lanora smiled broadly at her. "Have you met Florenz yet, Miss Marjory?" she asked with a mischievous look on her face.

Marjory assumed Florenz was another housemaid, or perhaps a kitchen maid. "No, I have not. Does she work with you and Anna?"

"She?" Lanora said and giggled. "Why, Florenz is a houseboy. A handsome one."

"Oh, of course! I should have known. I will keep my eye out for a handsome houseboy and let you know when I have met him," she said and smiled at Lanora. "Well, you better return to your chores. Wouldn't want to make Missus Simmons upset."

Lanora giggled again and nodded, and Marjory watched her as she slipped out of her room and down the narrow servants' staircase.

Chapter Three

Summer afternoon—summer afternoon; to me those have always been
the two most beautiful words in the English language.

HENRY JAMES

SPRING & SUMMER 1895
GLEN EYRIE

AS THE WEEKS PASSED, the girls began to feel more and more at home
at Glen Eyrie. Dorothy and Marjory, especially, enjoyed the fine
Colorado weather. The sun shone brightly nearly every day, and they
had little by way of rain. They spent hours roaming the grounds,
visiting the greenhouses, and meeting all of the servants.

Marjory particularly loved visiting Louis Zender, the dairyman. He
was from Switzerland, and he loved to yodel to the cows as he milked
them. The soothing sound, he claimed, made the cows' udders supple,
which, in turn, produced the freshest milk. Marjory pictured Louis, high

on a mountaintop in the Swiss Alps, yodeling his heart out to a group of cows, and it made her giggle.

They had had many cows at Loseley Park, but things were very different back in England. It would not have been deemed proper for a young lady to speak with the dairyman, let alone allow him to teach her how to milk a cow. But Marjory seized the opportunity and, after a few tries, became very proficient at milking.

"Ah, there you are!" Elsie shouted as she and Dorothy came around the corner of the barn one afternoon to see Marjory seated on a low stool, her hands grasping tightly to udders. An odd sight for their sweet, delicate sister. "What are you—?"

"Louis is teaching me how to milk!"

Elsie looked at Louis, then back at Marjory, who pleaded with her eyes to allow her to stay.

"That is very kind of you, Mister…?"

"Zender. Mister Louis Zender, at your service," he replied.

"Pleased to meet you," Dorothy said as she stuck out a hand.

Elsie looked surprised at Dorothy's enthusiasm and said, "I will just leave you to it, then, Marj? Dos?"

Her sisters just smiled, and Dorothy sat down on a second low stool.

Billie Burghardt and Carl Faun, the talented gardeners who tended Father's three greenhouses, filled them to the brim with not only flowers but also fruits, vegetables, and herbs. Every day, Elsie walked down to the greenhouses, and Billie allowed her to choose the flowers for the breakfast table. He had many varieties she had not seen since leaving England. Her favorite, though, was a small, purple flower with pointy petals and a soft yellow center.

"What is this one called?" she asked him one day. "I have seen it growing wild in the hills above the house."

"That one? Its proper name is *aquilegia*. But they call it Columbine."

"May I?" she asked.

Billie nodded his head and handed her a pair of gardening shears. She snipped a few stems, and Billie wrapped them in brown paper for her.

"Thank you, Billie!" she said. "This will brighten up my little windowsill rather nicely."

"PLEASE ALLOW ME TO introduce my wife," Berty said as a dark-haired woman with large, bright eyes stepped up next to him.

Since the Palmer girls' arrival, he had been eager to introduce Dorothy and Marjory to his wife and children and to give them a tour of their modest house near the front gate.

The girls shook her hand, and she whispered something to her husband.

"Yes, yes!" he said, and his wife scampered into the house.

She returned a few moments later with two children in tow. They had the same large eyes as their mother.

"Please meet my daughters," she said.

The oldest girl, who was not more than six years old, stepped forward to offer her hand, but the youngest hid in her mother's skirt and could not be coaxed out.

"You will meet her another time, maybe. She is very shy," Berty explained.

"Come here, beautiful," Marjory crouched down and opened her arms to the little girl.

The little girl peeked out from behind her mother's skirt and stared at Marjory, who pulled a few small chocolates from her reticule and held them out for her. The little girl rushed forward to accept the candy, and her big sister did the same. Marjory patted her curly head.

"You are very good with children," Berty observed.

"Marjory always seems to have children crowding around her skirts," Dorothy remarked. "Even when she was just a child herself. They listen to her."

Marjory did not hear them; she was busy teaching the Bertolotti girls her favorite hand-clapping game. Dorothy smiled at her sister.

"WHY ARE YOU DRESSED like that—?" Dorothy began.

She had entered the breakfast room moments before to find Father, Elsie, and Marjory enjoying eggs and sausage. Elsie, dressed in her finest gown, appeared ready to attend an opera or perhaps church.

"Dos!" Elsie cut across her and motioned for her to sit down. "There you are. Come join us."

"Please close the door," Father said. They could hear Mrs. Simmons and Berty out in the hallway, discussing some matter in raised voices.

Dorothy took a seat next to Marjory, who smiled at her with that knowing smile.

"You seem awfully chipper this afternoon, Elsie," Dorothy remarked. "And dressed in finery. Are we expecting company?"

"No," Father said. "I am taking Elsie into town to meet some of her old friends for tea at the Antlers."

Dorothy looked at Marjory and then back at Father. "The what?"

"Oh, my darling, I do apologize. I forget sometimes you are new to town." Father smiled, and Dorothy rolled her eyes.

"The Antlers is Father's hotel," Elsie explained. "It is the most luxurious resort hotel in the West, isn't that right, Father?"

"Well-l-l," Father said gruffly. "I suppose it is, but you make me sound like a prig."

"I do no such thing. Even Dorothy can appreciate luxury."

Dorothy shot her a dead-pan look, but Elsie was busy pouring another cup of tea.

"I thought you and Marjory might like to explore a little on your own while we are in town," Father continued.

"Brilliant idea, Father," Marjory replied.

Dorothy looked a little less convinced but acquiesced all the same.

"If you leave the house, do not wander far," Father urged. "Tell Missus Simmons where you intend to go, and check in with her when you have arrived back at the house."

"Yes, Father," Marjory said. "We will."

An hour later, Marjory and Dorothy waved at Father and Elsie as the carriage pulled away from the house.

"So," Marjory said and turned to her sister. "What should we do?"

Dorothy looked up at the sky for a moment and then back at Marjory and said, "I have an idea."

She turned on her heels and ran upstairs quickly; Marjory struggled to keep up but said nothing. Dorothy opened and closed doors, in search of something, until she reached the final door at the end of the hall. She swung it open to reveal Lanora making the bed.

"There you are!"

"Yes, Miss Dorothy?" Lanora said in surprise.

"Are you busy?"

"Well, I have to finish this bed here, and then I take my lunch with the other servants downstairs."

"If we help you with the bed, can you help us with something?"

"Alright, I suppose." Dorothy and Marjory grabbed a corner of the sheets, and the three of them finished making the bed in record time.

"Now, Lanora," Dorothy said. "I often see you descend the narrow staircase in the middle of the hallway. Where does it lead?"

Lanora looked confused. "Downstairs, of course. To the servants' area."

"Yes, of course," Dorothy replied, disappointed. "What I really want to know is, are there any *hidden* passages that are not detectable with the naked eye? Any secret staircases or tunnels or such?" She thought of the low passageway she had seen in the carriage house.

At Loseley Park, searching for hidden passages was Dorothy and Marjory's favorite pastime on rainy days. The Park had been built in the 16th century, during a time when servants were never to be seen, so it had countless hidden doors, false walls, and dark tunnels. A whole section of a wall in the library could be swung open to gain access to a "safe room" the original owners had built.

"This is not a castle, Dos," Marjory said. "Father and Mama built this house. They had no need for such secrecy."

"There is the storage closet on the second floor, and the hidden closet in Master Palmer's den ... I know!" Lanora said suddenly. "The rock tunnel. I suppose you could consider that hidden. I can show it to you, if you like."

A rock tunnel! That must have been what I saw the day we arrived, Dorothy thought.

"Perfect!" she replied.

"Follow me." They trailed behind Lanora as she led them down the servants' staircase to the lower floor near the kitchen. They could hear servants bustling about in there, already preparing the evening's supper.

Lanora led them outside and across the courtyard to another door that led into the butler's pantry. She showed them a small, low door. "Through there. That leads down to the carriage house."

"Yes! This must be what I saw. A footman had opened a door in the side of the hill by the carriage house and vanished. Seems odd to have a tunnel like this. I wonder why Father built it?" she said and looked at Marjory, who appeared slightly panicked.

"Perhaps he wanted the servants to have access to the carriage house during inclement weather?" she replied.

"Perhaps." The wheels in Dorothy's mind began to spin with thoughts of secret meetings and potential danger. She stuck her head far into the tunnel and paused.

"You do not plan to go down there, do you, Dos?" Marjory exclaimed.

"No," she replied and pulled back. But she longed to know the answer. Father and Elsie were not due back until supper. She could not wait that long. She knew who would know the answer: Berty.

"Follow me," she said. They left Lanora to enjoy her lunch and returned to the main part of the house. They found Berty sitting in Father's den, his feet propped up on a tufted footstool. He jumped up when they came in.

"Excuse me, misses! I did not expect to see you girls before supper." He looked embarrassed and began to tidy up the den. "Your father allows me to relax in here while he is out of the house." The servants would never have been allowed to relax in England, let alone relax in one of the master's private rooms. America was a strange place, indeed.

"Do not let us bother you, Berty, we only wanted to ask you a question."

"In that case, permit me to call for tea. We can sit in here, and you can ask me any questions you like."

The three of them made small talk for a few minutes until Anna delivered a teapot of black tea for the girls and a small carafe of black coffee for Berty. He poured the tea into two cups for them and leaned back in his chair, nursing his coffee. Dorothy felt shocked by this informality, but she knew Father would not object.

"Berty, you have been the butler here for many years," Dorothy began.

"Yes, I have," he replied.

"I wonder, what do you know about the rock tunnel that leads out from your pantry?"

He did not appear fazed by Dorothy's admission of being in the butler's pantry uninvited.

"Your Father built the rock tunnel to ferry up baggage during snow storms and such. And to keep you girls safe, of course."

"Safe? From what?" Marjory asked, her eyes wide with curiosity.

"Safe from kidnapping," Berty replied. "In the early years of your father's railroad career, he wanted to expand south through the Royal Gorge, but a rival railroad fought him tooth and nail. They wanted control of the gorge. The dispute lasted years, and your father received numerous death threats. Elsie was a young girl at the time, so he built the rock tunnel as a way to escape if ever someone came to Glen Eyrie with ill intentions."

"I never knew," Dorothy said.

"Eventually, your father won control of the gorge, but the death threats did not stop," Berty continued. "He feared greatly for your family's safety. Although he would never say it, I believe that is a big part of the reason your father stepped down from the railroad company. He could not bear the thought of something happening to his family. "

Dorothy looked across at Marjory, who lowered her eyes. If they had learned anything since coming to Colorado, it was that there was much they did not know about Father. They realized now they had never truly known him, when they were separated by an ocean.

"Any more questions, misses?"

"Not today, thank you," Dorothy said and the two girls left Berty in the den to enjoy the rest of his break.

DOROTHY AND MARJORY EXPLORED the house from top to bottom that day. They discovered a few more nooks and crannies that reminded them of the Park and got scolded by Mrs. Simmons for attempting to climb the steep ladder to the roof. She urged them to go outside and enjoy the sunshine for a while.

"Have fun, girls!" Mrs. Simmons called after them. "If you happen to go on the trail up above the house, do not be alarmed if you see a gravestone. We are aware of its presence," she said and bustled off to resume her work.

Dorothy shot a quick glance at her sister, who gulped and looked terrified. Marjory hated all things scary or unusual. It was bad enough that Loseley Park was rumored to be haunted, and now this? How would she bear it?

"That settles it," Dorothy said, grabbed her sister's hand, and started leading her up the trail above the house. She had to see this.

When Marjory realized what Dorothy had in mind, she did not protest. *Dos will not let anything happen to me*, she thought. They climbed and climbed up the steep trail until they reached a vantage point overlooking the grounds below.

"Look, Dos!" Marjory exclaimed and pointed to a herd of bighorn sheep resting on an outcropping above them.

"And, oh, look! A garden!" she exclaimed again. Dorothy followed her gaze to a small, walled garden quite a distance from the main house. "I wonder who—"

"Let's keep going," Dorothy cut across her and marched on. She could guess who the garden belonged to, but she did not want to think about that now. They were on the hunt for a grave.

As Dorothy led Marjory even higher up the hill, she began to think Father had left out a lot in his letters to her all those years. *A secret tunnel? And now a mysterious gravestone? What other mysteries would they uncover?*

As they rounded a bend in the trail, they spotted a clearing surrounded by scrub oak and a rounded gravestone peeking up from the dusty, dry ground. As they approached it, Dorothy squatted down and used her sleeve to wipe away what looked like years of dirt and grime. Soon the faded carvings became legible:

Here lies Charlotte Clark
Beloved wife, mother, grandmother
1873

Marjory gulped again. "Who is Charlotte Clark, Dos?"
Who indeed? Dorothy thought. "I have no idea," she replied.

Question after question rolled around in Dorothy's head. *Why would she be buried here and not in a cemetery?*

After a few more moments in front of the gravesite, Marjory moaned and said, "I am frightened, Dos. Let us go back."

"Alright. This place is a bit eerie, I will admit it."

They turned and started to make their way back down the hill to the house below. Feeling invigorated from their hike, Dorothy began to run, her long, brown hair whipping behind her in the strong breeze. As she rounded a bend in the trail, she hurtled headlong into another person.

"Oh! Pardon me, sir, I did not mean—"

As he straightened up and dusted off his jacket, she noticed he was a boy, not much older than she was. "Quite alright, miss." He patted his chest and arms, and with a small smirk, he said, "No broken bones."

"Of course you have no broken bones, I was not running very fast,"

Dorothy said, feeling slightly annoyed by his impertinence.

The boy chuckled, amused by Dorothy's very serious face. Marjory reached them then, and the boy bowed slightly. "Florenz Ordelheide, at your service."

Understanding dawned on Dorothy, and she felt embarrassed for not guessing who he was, for Marjory had informed her of the existence of the mysterious, handsome houseboy. He had a boyish grin, bright eyes, and a stylish haircut. He looked to be about 17 or 18, in the prime of young adulthood. He appeared every bit as handsome as Lanora had said, but Dorothy had been too flummoxed to notice before.

Marjory lunged for his hand, shook it rather forcefully, and said, "I am Marjory, the Master's youngest daughter."

"Pleased to make your acquaintance."

"And this is Dorothy—"

"*Miss* Dorothy Palmer," she cut across Marjory. "You are the houseboy, are you not?"

Florenz looked pleased. So she *had* heard of him. "Yes, miss," he said, "I work for your father. I hope that fact will not prevent us from being friends."

"Most certainly not!" Marjory nearly yelled.

"That is a bit presumptuous, but ... perhaps not," Dorothy replied and smiled at him.

"Thank goodness," he said.

Marjory leaned close to her sister and whispered something in her ear. "You ask him," Dorothy replied, but Marjory shook her head violently.

"It appears my sister has been stricken dumb—"

"By my excellent good looks," Florenz finished for her.

Dorothy shot him a look that said, "Not exactly," and played along as Marjory's mouthpiece. "My sister wonders if you might know anything about the gravestone at the top of this crest."

"Of course I do."

"Naturally. Well, would you be so kind as to share the

information?"

"For a price," he responded and winked at Marjory.

Marjory blushed and said, "The name on the gravestone. Who was she?"

"Rumor has it, she was some relation of yours. She was out visiting Glen Eyrie and fell down dead, just like that," he said and snapped his fingers. "Rumor also has it, she can be seen roaming the hills during the summer months, crying out for her lost child ..."

"That is nonsense!" Dorothy exclaimed. "The gravestone said she was a 'beloved grandmother.' Marj, do not listen to him."

Florenz burst into laughter then, and so did Dorothy. Marjory, however, giggled uncomfortably. "So none of that was true?" she inquired.

"The bit about her roaming the hills, crying for her lost child, is not true. The rest of it, I have on good authority, is the God-honest truth."

Recovered from her laughing fit, Dorothy looked up and squinted into the sun. "It feels late. We should get back."

"It is precisely four thirty in the afternoon," Florenz said with absolute confidence. Dorothy scanned the front of his vest for the outline of a pocket watch but found none.

"How do you—"

"Know the time? The position of the sun, of course." He looked up at the sky and then back down at them. "You can tell a lot from the sun."

Dorothy looked at him full in the face then. *He is a funny one,* Dorothy thought and smiled at him.

"I best get back, too, Miss Dorothy, Miss Marjory," he said and bowed. "But I hope to bump into you again ... soon." He nodded and smiled, then turned his back to them and hurried down the path towards the house.

The sisters stared at his retreating figure then linked arms and continued down the path after him. Neither of them spoke. Marjory felt excited by the presence of such an attractive and engaging young man in their midst. Dorothy, however, recognized a kindred spirit.

WHEN THEY RETURNED FROM their walk, they found Mrs. Simmons tidying up Father's den. They watched her for a moment, the way she gently fluffed the pillows and straightened the various stacks of books. She respected—and maybe even loved—Father, they could tell. They turned to each other and smiled before Dorothy broke the silence.

She knocked lightly on the doorframe. "Missus Simmons?"

The housekeeper turned at the sound of her name. "There you girls are. Pleasant walk? Come, come, have a treat." She herded them out of Father's den and closed the door behind them. The threesome stepped into the kitchen, where Mrs. Simmons bent to pick up a tray containing a pitcher of lemonade and lollipops for the girls.

She led them to the Music Room, deposited the tray, and turned to leave.

"Do not go, Missus Simmons," Marjory said. "Please. There is something I would like to ask you."

Mrs. Simmons looked unhappy for a moment but acquiesced and sat down near them. Marjory poured a tall glass of lemonade and held it out for her. Mrs. Simmons sipped the lemonade for a moment and then said, "What is it?"

Marjory turned to look at Dorothy, who raised her eyebrows in confusion. She could not imagine what her sister wanted to say.

"Would you—" she started, then looked down at her fidgeting hands. "Would you be so kind … as to help us?"

"Of course, child."

Marjory looked again at Dorothy for support, but Dorothy only smiled a little and nodded her head.

"Well, you see, sometimes I think I can remember this place. The way the red spikes reach towards the heavens and the curvature of the grand staircase and Father's den full of his war medals. But the truth is, the memories are not my own. They are cobbled together from years of Father's letters and Mama's stories.

"I have tried to remember, but I cannot. And it pains me—" Marjory stopped abruptly and reached for her handkerchief.

Dorothy looked sad as she said, "I, too, cannot remember much.

Bits and pieces, like flashes of time. Or beginnings and endings but never the middle. But what help can Missus Simmons give us?"

"She can help us remember," she replied and turned to Mrs. Simmons. "Would you? Please, tell us what we should know."

Mrs. Simmons looked at them each in turn and nodded her agreement. "Where to begin?" she said to no one in particular. "Ah, I know. We must start with your mama."

For the next hour, Mrs. Simmons told them everything. About their parents' hard work building Colorado Springs, Father's railroad ventures, Mama's little schoolhouse in town, and the day they completed Glen Eyrie. She told them about the railroad wars, Mama's sisters and brothers, and her illness.

That last bit was of particular concern to both girls. They knew Mama had taken the three of them to New York first, hoping the lower elevation would ease her pain, but, after two hard winters there, she could not bear another one. England's damp air and mild winters seemed like the best solution.

Dorothy and Marjory asked Mrs. Simmons question after question until their family history began to feel like their own. What before had been a story here and a story there became a timeline stretching back many years.

Finally, things began to make sense to Dorothy and Marjory: why Mama took them to England, why Father stayed behind, his blinding passion for this town, Mama's dream of a castle to call home. All of it.

After the hour was up, Mrs. Simmons had a surprise to show them. "Would you like to see your old room?"

Adjacent to Father's room, tucked into the corner, Mrs. Simmons swung open the door to reveal a rounded room with a large bank of tall windows. A fireplace sat in one corner, and the room was covered with flowered wallpaper. The memories washed over the girls like a tidal wave. The nursery looked exactly as they had left it: an iron crib in one corner, a rocking chair near it, a bookshelf, and a big basket of toys and dolls.

Father kept it all exactly the same, Dorothy thought. *But why?*

The sisters stepped forward into the room. It had recently been cleaned; a faint scent of lemons hung in the air. Marjory lightly stroked the crib bedding, and Dorothy sank into the well-worn rocking chair. They sat in silence for several minutes, taking it all in. Out of the corner of her eye, Marjory spied a shock of red hair sticking up out of the toy basket. She gave it a slight tug and lifted out a dilapidated, one-eyed doll.

"Is that—?" Dorothy began.

"Sally," Marjory moaned and buried her face into the doll's matted hair. "This was my favorite doll. I remember her."

Dorothy stood up from the rocking chair and placed a hand on her sister's shoulder. Just then, they heard footsteps on the staircase landing.

"Girls?" Father said. "Are you in here?" He stuck his head in the nursery door and looked surprised to find them there.

"We were just, uh—"

"It is alright, darlings," he said. "You do not need to explain." He looked back at Mrs. Simmons, who curtsied slightly and left.

As he turned back to her, Marjory explained, "Missus Simmons was kind enough to show us in, Father."

She could not decipher the look on his face. Was he angry? Sad?

"Father?" she said, but he continued to stare into the distance. "Father?" Marjory said again, louder this time.

He jumped slightly, his reverie broken. "I-I'm sorry, darling. What were you saying?"

"Is everything alright?" Dorothy asked, concerned.

"Yes. Yes, of course. I was merely lost in thought."

The girls stared at each other for a few moments. Then Dorothy said, "The nursery, Father, why did you never change it?"

Marjory understood the look on his face now: sadness.

"Girls," he began and sat in the rocking chair. He cleared his throat and rubbed his eyes. Dorothy and Marjory looked at him eagerly as he continued, "This is difficult for me to discuss with you."

"You do not have to—" Dorothy started.

"I want to," he replied. "It is time."

He cleared his throat and began, "After you left for England, the nursery became completely silent. No more laughter, no more children running about. The loss sent me into a dark depression like none I had experienced before. It was as if my heart had been pried from my chest. My only comfort was knowing you were safe and happy with Mama.

"After a year or so, Missus Simmons implored me to sort through your belongings and donate them to the orphanage, but I refused. I could not accept the fact that you were not coming back. In fact, we argued and I sent her away. I came to my senses a few hours later and begged her to return. We agreed to keep the door to the nursery shut at all times."

Father looked intensely pained by these memories, but he continued, "I wanted there to be something for you to remember. Just as it was. After we sealed the room, I had to rely on my memories instead. Sometimes, I would stand in the middle of the hallway outside of this room and close my eyes to listen for your sweet laughter. Poor Missus Simmons, I think she feared I was going mad. I thought I was, too. I know now that it was grief that led me to behave so. It made me happy to hear your little voices and to remind myself how much you loved it here. You did love it, girls—" he said and stared at them.

"Father, we were terribly sad without you," Marjory responded. "We talked about you all the time, and Elsie read your letters aloud to us in the evenings after supper. You were never far from us."

Dorothy stared at Father for a long moment and then smiled.

"DID YOU SEE RUTHIE Brunswick while you were there, darling?" Father asked Elsie. The four Palmers sat around the dinner table. Elsie had spent another day at the Antlers, but this time Father had not joined her. Now, naturally, he wanted to know all about it. "How about Thomas Millworth and the twins? I cannot remember their names—"

"Pudgy and Lucy," Elsie answered.

"Who names their child Pudgy?" Dorothy asked and laughed.

"I believe her real name is Patricia or Priscilla or something of that nature," Elsie said.

"She must have been a large child then, no?" Father asked and chuckled loudly, and Dorothy and Marjory burst into laughter.

Dorothy noticed Elsie was not joining in on the fun and said, "Oh, do not be so serious, Els. It was just a little joke."

"I know that," she replied and cracked a small smile.

"Anyway, Father," she continued, "I did see Ruthie and the Millworth siblings, along with Rowena Bell."

"Oh, did you indeed see Rowena?" Father exclaimed. "She would be a wonderful friend for you."

Rowena's father was a renowned physician and one of Father's oldest friends. They had met on a railroad surveying trip after the war. When Father chose to settle down in Colorado, Dr. Bell followed suit. He married a fine woman named Cara and built Briarhurst Manor in nearby Manitou Springs.

"Doctor Bell, he was your business partner, was he not, Father?" Marjory asked.

"Yes, Bell was my right-hand man when I founded the D and RG."

"And the Bell children and I used to be playmates," Elsie said.

"Yes, and Mama's youngest siblings, as well, darling," Father replied. "You spent many a lovely afternoon with the Bell children."

"What happened to Doctor Bell?" Dorothy asked.

"He and his wife and their younger children moved back to England after we sold the companies, I am afraid. About five years ago."

"Oh. I am sorry."

"Don't be, darling. He was a good friend. And now I have the pleasure of the acquaintance of his daughter, who keeps me informed of his every move," Father said and winked at them.

"I do believe Rowena is the loveliest girl in all of Colorado Springs, Father," Elsie declared. "Now that she is twenty-one, the eligible bachelors will be lining up to court her." Elsie paused.

Father leaned over and lightly brushed her cheek. "As they will be for you, darling. Wait and see."

Anna and Lanora cleared the dinner plates and laid fresh silverware and smaller plates for their dessert: chocolate mousse.

As Anna leaned next to Father, he said, "I asked Cook to make extra for the servants. Please see to it that everyone takes a proper break and enjoys the mousse."

"Thank you, sir."

"Father!" Elsie exclaimed after the servants had left. "You really are too dear."

He looked slightly sheepish as he replied, "Before you girls came back, the servants were all the family I had. I would not want to change that now."

"No, indeed."

Marjory kicked Dorothy under the table, and Dorothy shot her a quizzical look. "The grave—" Marjory began.

"Oh! Yes, *ahem*," Dorothy cleared her throat and turned to look at Father. "Father," she said and paused.

Father, engrossed in his mousse, merely replied, "Yes?"

"Who—who is Charlotte Clark?"

Father's eyes widened for a moment, but then he laughed out loud. "I knew you would find that one of these days!"

"Find what?" Elsie looked confused.

Dorothy ignored her and continued, "Why are you laughing?"

"Because, darling, you look terribly serious," he replied. When he noticed his daughters, especially Marjory, were not joining in on the fun, he cleared his throat and said, "She was Mama's grandmother."

"But I thought she lived in New York?" Dorothy asked.

"She did live in New York, but she came to Colorado on a visit, many years before you were born, when Mama and I were still only newly married. She had been an adventurer herself, when she was young, traveling by covered wagon to explore the West."

"But why is she buried here?"

"Buried!" Elsie exclaimed. "Now you *have* to tell me what is going on."

"During her visit," Father continued, ignoring Elsie, "she died quite unexpectedly. Mama considered burying her in the cemetery in town, but she knew her grandmother would enjoy being buried in a beautiful place with a view. Thus, on the crest behind the house."

Marjory looked wide-eyed in astonishment, while Dorothy felt completely intrigued. Father recognized Dorothy's excitement and felt a twinge of camaraderie with his wild child.

"That is very gothic of you. Why did I never know about this?" Elsie asked.

"I suppose your mama thought it would upset you."

"And she was right," Dorothy said, low enough for Marjory alone to hear her.

After they finished their dessert, they made their way to the fireside. Elsie and Marjory struck up a game of cards.

Father leaned over and said to Dorothy, "Dos, how would you enjoy a ride tomorrow? After breakfast?"

For the first time in three months, Dorothy smiled as she replied, "Do you mean it? Oh, I long for a ride. I have not had a proper one since before ... well, since before Christmas."

"Excellent," Father replied. "I have something I want to show you."

"GUESS WHO *I* MET today?" Florenz said teasingly as he and the Knight sisters took their supper in the servants' area.

Anna and Lanora stared blankly for a few seconds, then Anna said, "Well, aren't you going to tell us?"

"I met the misses today."

"All three?" Lanora asked.

"The younger two only. Miss Dorothy and Miss Marjory."

"What did you think of them?" Anna asked.

"They seem to be very elegant. Kind. Well-spoken," he said. "It was odd, though."

"What was odd?" Anna turned to him and looked intently at his face.

"They had just found the grave, and Miss Marjory looked so pale, like she had seen a ghost." He paused. "But it was I who had seen a ghost."

Anna looked at her sister, confused.

"I was looking at them, and their mother was staring back at me, in double vision."

"Do not be so dramatic, Florenz," Anna dismissed him with a wave of her hand.

"Truly! They are the same!"

"You never met their mother," Anna replied. "You were a little boy when they left. You did not even live here yet."

Florenz considered for a moment and then said, "Have you not seen the photographs scattered all throughout the house? There are probably a hundred of Queen."

"You are impertinent! Calling her 'Queen.' Do not let Missus Simmons or Berty hear you—they will ring your neck!" Anna exclaimed.

"Nevertheless. I, on the other hand, look nothing like my mother. In fact, there was a rumor—"

Anna socked him hard on the shoulder.

"Ouch! What was that for?"

Anna stared at him and motioned to Lanora. Florenz started laughing—a big belly laugh that prompted Cook to stick her head around the door.

"He is fine, Cook. Sorry to disturb you," she said and kicked Florenz under the table.

THE NEXT MORNING DAWNED bright and beautiful, with not a cloud in the sky. Elsie and Marjory made plans to explore the rose garden while the others took their ride. After breakfast, they made their way in that direction, and Father sent Dorothy upstairs to change into her riding habit.

Upon entering her room and seeing what must be her habit spread across the end of the bed, Dorothy became very confused.

"This is not my habit," she said to herself. She stepped into the hallway just as Anna passed by with a pail of firewood. "I believe you laid out the wrong habit, Anna. This looks to be made for a man."

Anna peeked her head around the corner to have a look at the offending habit. "No, Miss Dorothy, your Father had this one special made for you," she replied.

Dorothy held the habit up to the light. It appeared to be a gown-like coat on top, but the bottom resembled men's trousers.

What was he thinking?

She hesitatingly allowed Anna to assist her in getting dressed. The fabric felt odd around her legs, and she wondered how she would ever mount her sidesaddle. She spun around to get a look at herself in the mirror and was surprised by what she saw. She looked rather pretty.

Dorothy thanked Anna and descended the stairs to meet Father outside the front door. He sat atop his imposing black stallion, while Jesse, the head groom, held the reins to a beautiful chestnut mare.

As she stepped forward, Father said, "Her name is Lavender. She is for you."

Dorothy looked both shocked and a little embarrassed as she took the reins from Jesse. "Absolutely stunning creature," she said and brushed the mare's mane gently. Jesse placed a low step stool next to Lavender and motioned to Dorothy to assist her up.

Father noticed her look of confusion and said, "You will not be riding sidesaddle today, Dos. Colorado girls ride the same way as boys."

"But Father—"

"You can do it, Dos. Allow Jesse to show you." Jesse stepped onto the stool, placed his left foot in the stirrup, and swung his right leg up and over the horse.

"See?" Jesse said. "Piece of cake."

Dorothy felt a little apprehensive, but in truth she had always wanted to sit astride her horse like a man. After Jesse descended, she slipped her high-laced boot into the stirrup, then pulled with all her might and swung her leg over Lavender and into the stirrup on the opposite side.

"I did it!" she exclaimed.

"Perfect form, miss," Jesse said and winked at her. Dorothy felt herself blush at Jesse's remark. No English groom had ever acted so informally with her. She rather liked it.

Jesse handed Dorothy the reins and patted Lavender gently on the hindquarters. Father led them away from the house and west towards the foothills. As they rode, Dorothy began to spy a gap in the tall cliffs surrounding the property—a canyon hidden from view. Father looked handsome on his horse, she noted, so sure and confident in his stride.

He belongs here, Dorothy thought. *Much more than I ever knew.*

They approached the entrance to the canyon, and Father led them across a low stream. The edges of the canyon seemed to close in on them, and she feared they would be trapped. But Father knew the way well and confidently led them on.

After several minutes, the stream began to run faster, and Dorothy heard what sounded like crashing waves. It reminded her of the English coast—they had visited it many times. She could hear the waves roll up onto the shore and crash against the seawall in her mind. As they approached the noise, she saw that it came from a large waterfall surrounded by pine trees with a small, clear pool beneath.

"How marvelous!" she shouted to Father above the noise.

He turned around in his saddle to look back at her and waited as she rode up next to him. "This was your mother's favorite place. Dorothy Falls."

Dorothy stared at her father for a few seconds until she felt hot tears begin to pool in the corners of her eyes. She blinked them back and cleared her throat.

"She told me—" she started and then paused to collect herself. "She told me she named her favorite spot after me, but I did not realize—. I did not realize."

Dorothy paused again and thought for a few moments before she asked, "Why me, Father? Why not Elsie Falls or Marjory?"

"Because you were her answer to prayer. Her miracle child."

Father began to tell Dorothy a story she had never heard but had always longed to know: the story of her birth. One time, when she was a little girl, she had asked Mama to tell her the story, but she looked so grieved that Dorothy never dared to ask again.

"When Mama was a few weeks away from your birth, Dos, we went riding in these foothills, like we did almost every day. But that day was different. Mama started to have trouble breathing. We stopped and I pulled Mama down from her horse and laid her on the ground. She gasped for air and clutched her heart. That was when I knew she was having another attack.

"We were not supposed to be out riding," Father continued. "Mama had suffered a major attack early in her pregnancy. The doctor had ordered her to stay in bed until you were born, but she begged for a ride. You know Mama, she hated being cooped up for any length of time. The falls were not very far away. I thought it would be alright to take a quick ride."

Father paused, lost in thought. "I believed I would lose her that day, that same hour," he continued. "But by the grace of God she started to breathe normally again. After a while, the pain subsided, and she was able to walk beside her horse the entire way back to the house. Not three weeks later, you were born. The doctor did not know whether you would survive, but you did. You are a fighter, Dos."

"But after that she got sick," Dorothy said quietly.

"After that your mama's health did decline. She stayed as long as she could, but eventually the doctor urged her to go to a lower elevation. We had to make a difficult decision, but she would not have survived had she stayed in Colorado," Father explained.

Dorothy looked pensive. She had many thoughts rolling around in her head, but one thought lingered at the front of her mind, begging to be released.

"Father," she began, "why did you remain in Colorado when we went away to England?"

Father appeared taken aback but responded in a gentle tone, almost as if he had been waiting for her to ask him. "I stayed behind because I wanted to make a life for us here. The day you all left was the very worst day of my life. I could not bear the thought that I had let you go. I even made up my mind to sell my companies and join you abroad, but then I had the dream."

"Dream?"

Father looked pensive again and then continued, "I dreamed of a beautiful city brimming with light and hope. The people in the city were happy; they were free. It was a safe haven in the midst of a nation in turmoil, a utopia at the foot of the Rockies. And I saw you, my family, full of joy and laughter. I knew I could not abandon that dream, even though it cost me so much."

Dorothy was surprised by Father's response. She expected him to make a futile excuse or to tell her it had been his duty to stay behind, but she recognized a common longing in her Father's heart: to make his mark on the world. She desperately longed for the same. For the first time, Dorothy began to realize he was much more than the father who broke her heart. When she looked at him now, she saw the dreamer.

They made their way back to the house in almost complete silence, but something had shifted. Instead of the normal, heavy air between them, Dorothy felt happy.

When they arrived back at the house, Mrs. Simmons had already ordered lunch to be laid. Dorothy felt her stomach clench; she had not realized how hungry she was. She desperately wanted to get out of her riding habit, so she made her way upstairs to her quarters. After removing her boots and stripping out of the habit, she looked at herself in the mirror above her washstand. She had dark circles under her eyes, but she also noticed she looked lighter, freer. She felt better than she had in a long time—at least since Mama died.

AFTER SUPPER, ELSIE STOLE away from the group and descended the steep hill beside the house to a small structure below—one-story and made of wood, with a low roofline and a wraparound porch. The old schoolhouse. Her favorite spot.

Ahhhh, Elsie breathed deeply as she sat on the stairs and laid her head back against the wooden pillar. She closed her eyes for a moment and let the memories wash over her.

Elsie had loved to spend time in here. So many happy memories of a childhood spent with Mama's brothers and sisters. She pushed off from her sitting position and climbed the small staircase to the wraparound porch.

During the warm months, Teacher would hold class on this porch. The children would observe the bighorn sheep and wild turkeys as they went about their studies. Sometimes, Teacher would take the children for a walk around the property, and they would dip their toes in the creek and climb small boulders. These outings would not be deemed "proper education" at an ordinary school, but to Teacher they were more educational than any textbook could be. Every day, Mama and Aunt Ellen would descend the small hill to bring milk and cookies to their children.

Elsie swung open the door and stepped inside. It looked much smaller to her now than she remembered it as a child. She could not now imagine how Teacher and several children had fit comfortably inside, let alone with desks and books and things.

She ran her fingers over the mantelpiece and opened the tall cabinets flanking its sides. Teacher used to store her materials inside, and she would carry a long key around her waist. Why she insisted on locking the cabinet was a mystery to Elsie and her aunts and uncles. They dearly longed to look inside but could only ever catch a glimpse of its contents.

One time, Aunt Maud had stolen Teacher's key and opened the cabinet while she had her back turned. The children had expected to find all sorts of secrets, but instead it was filled with schoolbooks and chalk, nothing else. How disappointed they all were.

Those were happy, carefree days. A childhood filled with wonder and excitement and lots of love. Everything was perfectly wonderful for a long time, and Elsie remembered those years as the best of her life thus far. But looking out towards Glen Eyrie in that moment, she felt a deep sense of joy and belonging and immense happiness to finally be home again.

Chapter Four

Autumn carries more gold in its pocket than all the other seasons.
JIM BISHOP

FALL & WINTER 1895
GLEN EYRIE

"ARE YOU READY FOR another adventure?" Father said animatedly as he looked around at his daughters. The night before, he had entered each of their rooms to say goodnight and announce his plan of a long horse ride to the "north country" promptly after breakfast the following day. The four of them sat around the table in their full riding regalia, minus their hats. Father had made it clear that they must leave as promptly as they could, so that morning, each of the girls had asked Anna and Lanora to help them into their habits rather than their normal day clothes.

"As ready as we possibly could be," Marjory replied and Father beamed at her.

"Then let us go!"

He led them to the front of the house, where Jesse and three grooms stood waiting to help them mount their steeds. Once atop, Father took off onto the gravel road leading out of the valley and onto the high path. They traveled north for some time, up and over steep foothills. He glanced behind him often to check on the girls' progress and to point out the "spectacular view of the peak from this spot."

A few miles into their journey, Elsie rode up alongside her father and asked, "Where *exactly* are we headed?"

In reply, he slowed his horse to a stop and jumped down. The others followed suit as Father unlatched a blanket and a basket from his saddle. Cook had prepared a scrumptious picnic lunch for them.

"As your sister has pointed out," Father said between bites, "I have been teasingly elusive about our destination up until now. Allow me to explain. We are headed to Husted." Father paused to take a swig of water.

Around 30 years previously, several pioneers had come to the valley by way of wagon trains in search of fertile land and opportunities. They built homesteads, planted wheat, raised cattle, and cut down wood in the nearby forests to be sold as lumber for booming Colorado Springs. Over time, the homesteaders named their small town Husted and, with Father's blessing, added a railroad station, a roundhouse, and a railroad bunk house.

As the girls had noted on their trip from Castle Rock to Colorado Springs, the summit of the steepest incline was nearly a thousand feet higher than the surrounding land. In order for Father's trains to successfully summit the incline, a helper steam engine would be added to the end of a line of train cars at the roundhouse in Husted. The helper engine would push the train to the summit, at which point it was detached, turned around, and traveled south back to Husted.

"Shall we continue on?" Elsie asked after they had had their fill of picnic lunch.

The four of them mounted their horses once again and rode the last few miles to Husted. The girls were surprised to see not only the railroad station and roundhouse but also a schoolhouse and a few shops. The townspeople waved at Father and the girls as they passed by. Father led them through town and west to a beautiful farmhouse in the middle of a cattle ranch.

They had not dismounted for more than a few seconds before the screen door opened and a tall man came out to greet them. "General Palmer," he said as he shot out a hand to shake Father's.

"How do you do, Mister Lehmann? Well, I hope." Mr. Lehmann nodded, and Father continued, "Allow me to introduce my daughters—Miss Palmer, Miss Dorothy Palmer, and Miss Marjory Palmer." Mr. Lehmann tipped his hat to them.

"Please, come inside," he said and led them to a pleasant sitting room. "I understand you have some business you would like to discuss," he turned to Palmer. "I wondered if your daughters would enjoy seeing Cathedral Rock?"

"I believe they would," Palmer responded.

"Wonderful. Then I will alert my stable boy, Robbie. He would be delighted to take you ladies there."

Father looked at his girls and said, "I will join you there once Mister Lehmann and I have discussed our business. Enjoy yourselves; it is quite beautiful."

They mounted their horses once again and followed Robbie away from the farmhouse. Not far away, on the edge of the cattle ranch, they came to a white rock formation over 100 feet tall. Elsie could easily see why it was given the name Cathedral Rock, for it inspired a deep sense of awe. As they approached, she noticed odd markings around the base of the formation. A closer look revealed dozens of names that had been etched into its sides.

She pointed out the names to her sisters and Robbie, who explained, "These are the names of the pioneers who settled this land. Fifty in all. My folks included."

Evans, Otis, Lennox, Bishop, Burgess, Capps, McAlroy, Lehmann … Husted.

"Calvin Husted, eighteen sixty-four," Marjory read. "He must have been the first one."

"He was," Robbie confirmed. "You will see many Bishops. That is my name. My father and several of his family members came West in the seventies."

How marvelous, Elsie thought, *to pack up your belongings, load them onto a wagon, and head West for an unknown land, battling the overwhelming fear of Indian attack, the ever-changing weather, the uncertainty of available land or a place to live upon arriving at their destination. It is no wonder they chose to settle in this valley. It is breathtaking.*

Father did not meet them at Cathedral Rock, as he had planned. When the party arrived back to the Lehmann ranch, he and Mr. Lehmann were still discussing their business. Elsie stepped in to remind Father of the late hour.

"We must leave soon if we want to make it home by nightfall."

Father only nodded and shook Mr. Lehmann's hand.

Back on the open road, the sun began to make its descent behind the mountains as they traveled south towards home. They arrived back to Glen Eyrie just as the final rays of sunshine crested the top of Pike's Peak and sunk below.

AS SEPTEMBER SLIPPED INTO October, Father took advantage of the unseasonably fine weather to show his daughters the incomparable beauty of a Colorado fall. Every morning, he pointed out the changing aspen trees on the mountainside and boasted of the impending winter snow.

"It will snow by All Hallows' Eve," he predicted.

Every opportunity they had, the four of them took long horseback rides during the crisp mornings and sat together by the roaring fire in the evenings, reading aloud and playing cards while Marjory entertained them on the piano.

One fine fall day in early October, Father and the girls rode to nearby Garden of the Gods. Wholly unlike the gardens in England, this was full of enormous, red, thin rocks that stretched into the sky, with Pike's Peak above; Major Domo and the other formations on the Glen Eyrie property were miniature in comparison. Being situated directly below the most attractive view of the peak gave the scene a postcard-like effect that was most pleasing to the girls. Father explained that the garden had served as a summer camp for the Ute Indians for hundreds of years—until government officials relocated the tribes to reservations.

A large farm was nestled among the spiked rocks, and as they rode up to the front gate, they noticed a hand-painted sign that read "Rock Ledge Ranch" with a small one below it: "Pumpkins for Sale." Dorothy spied the orange orbs lying in a field in the distance and squealed with excitement. Her sisters whipped around atop their horses to look at her; they had not seen her so excited in weeks.

The four of them dismounted, and Father led them up the wooden front steps to speak with the farmer's wife. He rapped lightly on the door, and a woman swung it open not a full beat later.

"General Palmer! To what do I owe the pleasure?" she exclaimed and then looked embarrassed. "Pardon me, sir, I watched you ride up. Please, do come in!"

"You are very kind, Missus Chambers, but we spotted your pumpkin sign and could not resist. Allow me to introduce my daughters, Elsie, Dorothy, and Marjory," he said.

"Very nice to meet you three," she said as she shook their gloved hands. "Please, call me Elsie." She winked at the oldest Palmer daughter.

A tall man wearing a wide-brimmed hat and coveralls came around the side of the house, dusting his hands on his pants as he walked. When he caught sight of Father, he two-stepped up the porch stairs and held out his hand.

"Robert! How are you, old friend?" Father said heartily and clapped him on the back. "I heard you had a wonderful harvest this year."

"Yes we did. In fact, we have so many pumpkins we do not know what to do with them. It is as if they are growing out of our ears. Poor

Elsie here has devised many recipes that include pumpkin, but I have to admit—I am getting rather sick of them!" He laughed and slapped his knee.

Normally, the Chambers raised cattle and had an extensive asparagus garden, but this year they wanted to try something a little different.

"I do apologize for coming unannounced like this," Father started. "I was telling Elsie that my girls spotted your pumpkins and became very excited."

"Follow me," the farmer said mischievously and ran down the porch steps. "I will show you the best beauties."

They followed him out to his furthest field, glancing around at their surroundings as they went. His farm was really quite perfect—situated at the base of the Garden of the Gods, providing shelter from the elements and ample shade for his more sun-adverse crops.

"This is absolutely idyllic," Elsie said to the farmer as they walked.

"I admit I do not know what that means, miss, but I thank you all the same," he replied and winked at her.

Elsie blushed and laughed a little to herself. "I just mean your farm is very beautiful." He tipped his hat and smiled at her.

They reached the outer field full of big, ripe pumpkins, and Father bent down to test their heartiness. He rapped his knuckles lightly on some of the biggest ones and pressed firmly into their thick skin. Dorothy thought briefly that perhaps Father was making a show of it for the farmer.

He stood back up and shook hands with Mr. Chambers. "Please deliver one-hundred to Glen Eyrie and another one-hundred to the children's home."

"As you wish!" the farmer said and clapped Father on the back.

The Palmers bid their adieus and mounted their horses to return home. When the pumpkins arrived at Glen Eyrie, the girls found a place for each throughout the property. Some of them they had carved into jack-o-lanterns to adorn the pathways and footbridges of Glen Eyrie; others they gave to Cook to make pumpkin soup and pumpkin cake; and still others they gave to the servants to adorn the mantelpieces in their quarters.

SINCE THEIR ARRIVAL IN Colorado, Elsie had received exactly zero letters from Leo. Despite promising to correspond, the letter box was empty. Marjory, ever the thoughtful one, inquired after him often, to which Elsie could only reply, "I have not had a letter in some time." Alas, she missed him.

She sat down at her writing desk, unscrewed her pen, and began to write. She intended to relay how well they were all settling in and how pleasant the voyage across the Atlantic had been, but she could not find the words. She found herself, instead, thinking about how much she missed him and how desperately she wished he could be with them there in Colorado.

She was happy here—blissfully so—and she wanted to share that happiness with him.

In the end, Elsie composed a letter that was equal parts cordial and warm. *Good enough for now,* she thought.

"I KNOW SOMETHING YOU don't know," Florenz sang and brushed Dorothy lightly on the nose.

She blushed but said nothing.

He fell backward over the couch in the library and kicked his long legs up over the arm. "Come on, then. Ask me what it is."

"Do not encourage him," Anna warned as she came into the room. She was carrying a long-handled duster.

From his upside-down position, Florenz's mouth dropped open in a mock "*Moi?*"

"Yes, you!" she replied and punched him on the arm.

He flipped his legs right-side up and nestled into the couch. "Miss

Elsie has a lover."

"Indeed? Well, I am not surprised. Elsie is beautiful and smart and charming," Anna replied, matter-of-factly.

"How do you know, Florenz?" Dorothy asked, surprised.

"Because I saw the letter. She called me into the library yesterday and handed me a letter addressed to a Mister Leopold Hamilton Myers, or some such mouthful of a name."

"I do not know what difference it makes to you," Dorothy reprimanded him. "But he is not a lover; he is her old friend."

"Same thing, is it not?" he said and locked eyes with Dorothy.

AS ALL HALLOWS' EVE approached, so too did the girls' annual birthday celebration. All three had birthdays within two weeks of each other—Dorothy's was first, on October 29th, then Elsie's on October 30th, and finally Marjory's on November 12th. When they were little girls, Father and Mama celebrated each birthday separately, but as the girls grew, they thought it would be enjoyable to have one big party to celebrate all three. The joint birthday tradition had started a few years ago, and the girls could not imagine it any other way. This year, Elsie would be turning 23, Dorothy, 15, and Marjory, 14.

The morning of their birthday celebration, Anna helped Marjory dress in her new frock—blue silk with intricate lace and beadwork. Mama had bought the silk a few years ago in Paris, and Father had the gown made up by the finest dressmaker in Denver. She wanted to look stunning at breakfast, even if only Father and her sisters would be present. "Start how you mean to go on," Mama used to say. *Mama*, she thought, *oh, how I wish you were here.*

After she finished dressing, she dismissed Anna and sat for a moment alone to think about Mama. Marjory believed Mama would be very proud of her if she were here. Six months ago, Marjory had been desperate to stay in England, but now she felt grateful for the time she had spent in Colorado. She felt stronger and more grown up than she ever had before and more at home in the Wild West than she thought possible. It surprised and delighted her. And she knew Mama would be so pleased.

Composing herself, and wiping a tear from her cheek, Marjory descended the stairs to find Father, Elsie, and Dorothy already seated in the dining room. Her sisters were also dressed in their finest frocks. Elsie wore a light pink one, which complemented her dark eyes. For Dorothy, an emerald green one that played nicely off of her flawless, ivory skin.

Marjory entered the room to "Oooh"s and "Aaaah"s from her sisters and a "You look absolutely beautiful, darling" from Father. She kissed them each in turn. Cook had prepared the girls' favorite breakfast: poached eggs, fried tomatoes, and baked beans—a true English breakfast. Elsie would have been happy with some oatmeal and hot tea, but she played along when she saw her sisters' eyes light up at the spread.

"Now, Marjory, I have a very important question to ask you," Father said with a wink. "Now that you are *old*, will you not try coffee?"

Marjory considered the invitation with much trepidation. A proper English lady would never drink black coffee. But a Western one would.

"Elsie and Dorothy both agreed to try it, and to my surprise and their utter shock, they enjoyed it immensely," Father said.

She nodded her approval, and Father poured her a steaming mug. He taught her how to add the right amount of cream and sugar to cut the bitterness.

She took a sip, swished it about in her mouth, and swallowed. It was delicious! The nutty flavor mixed perfectly with the warm cream. She was in heaven.

"Now you are a real Colorado girl," Father said.

Marjory looked around at her sisters and smiled.

"Today is a very special day," Father continued. "I have a surprise for you, and I think you are going to love it."

"He really loves surprises," Dorothy said to no one in particular.

Three hours later, they chugged into Pueblo. Years ago, Father had helped transform a dusty, old fort town into a thriving city by building a massive steel mill, which employed hundreds of workers and manufactured rails for Father's railway. Immigrants from southern Europe, Russia, and Asia flocked to the steel mill to find steady work with a decent wage.

"Are you taking us to the mill, Father?" Elsie asked. She turned to her sisters.

"No, not today. This is something far better."

At the train station, Father hired a carriage to convey them through town to a beautiful park on the north edge. As they rounded the bend into the park and the trees parted, they spied the outline of a large, opulent building with many oversized windows opposite a quaint pond.

"What is it?" Marjory asked.

"They call this the Mineral Palace," Father responded. "It was completed about four years ago and has done a splendid job of attracting tourists."

"I can imagine!" Marjory exclaimed. "It is beautiful."

As they walked into the oversized front doors, the girls marveled at the sight before them. The structure boasted domes and colonnades, murals of frontier life and important American citizens, and sculptures of the "Silver Queen" and "King Coal," sitting on their oversized thrones. The walls were lined with low shelves displaying the many types of minerals and gems being mined in Colorado: platinum, amethyst, opal, gypsum, iron, salt; the list went on and on.

"What are those?" Dorothy exclaimed.

They looked toward where she pointed—a real-life grotto complete with stalactites and stalagmites.

"This rivals the most magnificent palace in all of Europe, I am absolutely convinced," Elsie said excitedly.

As they walked around, many people began to recognize Father and came forward to be introduced. He presented his three daughters to them, and even the most fashionable among them were impressed with the girls' gowns, hairstyles, and jewelry. Dorothy thought she and her sisters must still have a foreign look about them, or perhaps the strangers were intrigued to find Father in the company of women. Whatever it was, it made Dorothy feel a sense of pride in her family.

"My dear General Palmer!" A tall, slender man of around 60 years of age, with a mustache and a large nose, pushed his way through the crowd that had gathered.

"McAllister, my good fellow, what are you doing in Pueblo?" Father said and clapped his old friend on the back.

"Same as you, I expect," Major Henry McAllister replied. "Magnificent place, is it not?" Noticing the three young women standing next to Father, he said, "Can it be? Can these lovely ladies be the famous Dorothy, Marjory, and Elsie?"

Father smiled broadly as he nodded his head.

"Miss Dorothy and Miss Marjory, you will not remember me, but I used to bring you taffy when you were girls. And Miss Elsie—you, too, have grown since your last visit out West. How delightful to see you all!"

"How are Mary and Matilda? And Missus McAllister?" Elsie asked as she shook his hand.

"Elizabeth is very well, thank you. The girls will be sad to have missed seeing you."

"And we, them. Please tell them they must come around for tea very soon."

"They will be delighted." Major McAllister noted the slightly confused look on Marjory's face and said, "I served with your father during the war. He was our fearless general." He winked at Palmer. "We grew up not forty miles from each other in Delaware and joined the cause around the same time. After the war, I followed your father out here to Colorado. And here we are."

"You left out the best part," Father replied. "Major McAllister did not simply follow me out to Colorado; he ran the Colorado Springs Company for me. We also founded *Out West* together. Our town would not be what it is today without the Major's dedication."

"*Out West?*" Dorothy asked.

"You know it as *The Gazette Telegraph*, but once upon a time it was a humble, once-weekly publication," Father explained.

"That reminds me, Palmer. I received a telegraph from Cornelius Vanderbilt. We have some decisions to make about the paper."

"I wondered when he would contact you," Father replied, gruffly. "I am not looking forward to that conversation. Let us discuss this together soon."

"By all means."

"Well, we had better head back north. Join us?"

Major McAllister nodded his approval, and Father had the carriage brought around for their departure to the train station.

After they boarded the train, Major McAllister left the compartment for a moment, and Dorothy asked Father, "Earlier, in the Palace, I thought I heard you say Cornelius Vanderbilt. Not *the* Cornelius Vanderbilt, grandson of the Commodore?"

"No, no. This man's name is Cornelius Vanderbilt Barton. Old McAllister is what you would call a bit charismatic, so he sometimes leaves off the 'Barton' when we discuss it in public."

"Oh. What business do you have with this man?" Elsie asked.

Father pondered for a moment before he replied, "Mister Barton is interested in buying our little newspaper. I thought I was ready to sell, but now I cannot decide if I have the heart to let it go."

LATER THAT EVENING, FLORENZ found Dorothy sitting cross-legged on the floor in the library, a new book—a leather-bound copy of *Oliver Twist*, a birthday present from Father—spread out across her lap. She looked up at him as he came in and smiled broadly. He smiled back with his boyish grin.

"If you keep reading like that your eyes will cross," he teased.

"Well, even if my eyes cross I will still be cleverer than you," she shot back, and Florenz laughed out loud.

He paused for a moment while Dorothy returned to her book.

"Come with me," he said and she looked up at him. "I have a

birthday surprise for you."

"But—"

He pressed a finger to his lips then took her hand to lift her out of a sitting position. Her new book tumbled to the floor. She bent down to pick it up, dusted it off, and laid it neatly on the table. She turned to look at him and reached out her hand to take his. He led her up the wooden staircase to the top floor, and from there they climbed the narrow spiral staircase to the tower room. Florenz slid open the door to a circular room. She noticed a few old toys and several large hooks hanging from the ceiling, with what looked like hammocks piled up in the center of the room.

Dorothy shivered as the cold air blasted her face. The tower room was open to the elements. Florenz wrapped his arm around her shoulders.

"This was where your mother's brothers slept during the warm summer months," he explained. "Your Father keeps this room closed off, but I found the key when I was cleaning the butler's pantry."

"Found it?" She laughed and nudged him in the ribs. "Stole it, more like."

"Maybe—" he said and grinned.

Leaving his warm embrace, Dorothy walked about the room, taking in the view of the grounds.

"This has the best view of any of the rooms in Glen Eyrie. I wonder why Father keeps it closed up?" Dorothy asked Florenz.

"I have often wondered that myself, but I figure he cannot bring himself to clean it out. He loved those boys so much. He became like a father to them when their own father died. And even though they are grown now, he still likes to remember them as children. Or so Missus Simmons used to say."

Dorothy looked pensive. Florenz came up next to her and placed his hands over hers.

"What is it, my—"

She looked quickly at his eyes and then down at the floor. *My what? Was he about to say "my love"?* she asked herself.

She ignored the awkward silence that had overtaken the room and said, "They are his sons, or as close to sons as he will ever have."

"Yes. But you are his daughter. His beloved daughter." He gently caressed her cheek.

She pulled away from his touch, embarrassed. "You are right, Florenz," she said. "I am being silly."

When she looked up at him, she saw a look in his eyes she had never seen before. Florenz looked eager, hopeful. Before she knew what was happening, he leaned down and kissed her. Dorothy pulled back in shock and stared at him.

"What are you doing, Florenz!?" she demanded.

"Oh, Dorothy! Please do not pull away. Don't you know how much I love you?"

"Love me? Florenz, what are you talking about?"

"I love you, Dorothy. Since the day I met you, I have loved you. I thought you knew," he said.

Dorothy looked utterly shocked. *Why is he doing this?* she thought. *He is going to ruin everything.*

She took a moment to compose herself and looked straight into Florenz's eyes.

"Florenz, you—you are my *friend*. I love you like a friend. Nothing more."

Florenz looked crestfallen, betrayed.

"We cannot … I cannot … it will not work, you and me," she tried to explain.

"You are wrong, Dorothy," he said and pressed his lips against hers again. She backed away and buried her face in her hands. She felt horrible, like her world was crashing in around her. *How could I have been so stupid?*

She could not bear to break Florenz's heart. "I am not ready," she started again. "But I could not bear it if this meant we can no longer be friends. I cherish your friendship so dearly."

Florenz looked slightly happier. He took her admission as a sign of uncertainty, rather than a closed door.

"Bet on *me*, Dos," he said and gently touched her face. "One day I mean to marry you."

What have I done? she thought.

As winter approached, the girls began to hunker down inside the house more, venturing out only on days when the temperature felt bearable. Wintertime in England had been cold, but in a different way than in Colorado—much more moisture and far less snow. On days when the sun shone, Dorothy and Marjory enjoyed bundling up to build a snowman or frolic for a bit in the snow—at least until it soaked through their boots and mittens. Often, Father would allow Lanora and Florenz to join them, a freedom they both enjoyed immensely.

On days when the weather was not fine, they played card games together by the fire until Lanora and Florenz had to return to their housework. After that, the girls would pursue their favorite pastimes. Elsie spent hours reading *Dombey & Sons*, Keats's love poems, and her new favorite, *Ramona*. Marjory practiced the piano tirelessly, and when asked about it, she said she wanted to "preserve her skills" and quickly changed the subject.

Dorothy, on the other hand, retreated inside herself and remained in a poor mood for weeks. In moments of clarity, she blamed it on the depressing weather and her rocky relationship with Florenz, but most days she could not understand why she felt so blue. Fall was her favorite season back in England, but she could not seem to rescue herself from gloomy thoughts.

Father began to notice something was wrong with Dorothy when she retired early to bed and lost her appetite for several days in a row. He called an emergency meeting with Elsie and Marjory to ascertain their opinions on the matter, but neither of them had any clue as to why Dos was so withdrawn. Then something came to mind that he was convinced would brighten her mood.

He asked Mrs. Simmons to summon Dorothy and Marjory to his

den, where he waited for them in his favorite armchair.

"Come in, girls, come in," he said after he heard a soft knock on the door.

Dorothy and Marjory entered and sat cross-legged on the floor, their backs to the fireplace.

"Did you know," he began. "Were you aware, that is—" He stopped and cleared his throat. "Your Mama dearly loved orphan children."

"Yes, Father," Marjory interjected. "She donated a portion of her income every month to the children's home near Loseley Park. She talked about the children often and was very concerned for their wellbeing."

"Yes," Father said. "You will not remember, but when Mama lived here at Glen Eyrie, every year at Christmastime she invited all of the local children to a party here at the house. All of the children, even those from the orphanage. For obvious reasons, I have not done it in many years. But this year, I want to throw the biggest party this town has seen," he said with a twinkle in his eye.

"Truly?" Marjory squealed with delight. "Oh, how I long for a party!"

"Truly, my darling, and I want you and Dorothy to organize it."

"YOU ARE GOING TO love this," Father said as they ascended the steep staircase leading to the big, oak front door of the orphanage. Father wanted the girls to see the orphanage in person, to get a sense of how the children lived.

The director met them just inside. The orphanage was quite dark but well-kept and orderly. The director led them to the dining hall, where the children were enjoying lunch during a break from classes. They appeared clean and tidy, although dressed in very plain clothes.

Dorothy's heart was moved by the sight of the children laughing together and playing games while they relaxed between lessons of arithmetic and spelling. They seemed happy, but she knew what turmoil they must be experiencing on the inside. Many of the children had left their homes in the East or the Midwest and traveled over a thousand miles for their parents to find treatment for consumption and solace in the clean air and abundant sunshine of Colorado. Too often, these treatments were in vain. Others had lost their fathers to accidents in the nearby mining town, and, unable to feed and care for them, their mothers had given them over to be wards of the state.

Dorothy was all too familiar with the sting of abandonment. With Father here in Colorado, and Mama dying, she had felt very alone back in England. Things were different now, but she would never forget the feeling of uncertainty and hopelessness that can pervade a child's mind.

Marjory approached a group of children and soon had them all laughing with her easy manner and silly jokes. Dorothy hung back for a moment, uncomfortable and awkward, but after seeing her sister's confidence, she stepped towards a small group of girls and said, "My name is Dorothy."

The girls stared at her with wide eyes, taking in her lovely dress and sparkling jewelry. She suddenly felt very self-conscious, almost selfish, for wearing such nice attire in their presence. Dorothy knew she could not save these little girls from the harsh world they lived in, but she could do something small to make their lives happy, if even for one day.

"How would you girls like to come to my father's house for a Christmas party?" she asked them.

"Do you mean it?" one of them asked.

"I do," Dorothy said and turned around to look at Father. He spoke animatedly to the director, who looked pleased by his visit. Dorothy waved Marjory over to where she sat, and the pair chatted with the orphan girls and gave them small trinkets—barrettes for their hair, a small broach, some sweets.

To his embarrassment, the director always treated Father like a king during his visits. He wished she would act normally around him, but he donated a large sum of money every year to this orphanage, and the director knew to make a good impression on him; its very livelihood depended on him.

After some time, Dorothy and Marjory bid goodbye to the children and promised to see them soon. As they walked out of the building and entered their carriage to head home, Father looked around at his daughters and smiled.

"What is it, Father?" Marjory asked him.

"It is nothing," he said and paused. "I just feel proud of you both. You were naturals in there."

"You taught us well, Father," Marjory replied.

BY MID-DECEMBER, DOROTHY and Marjory worked hard to put the finishing touches on their plans for the Christmas party. As it drew closer, they pulled Elsie into the planning, too. She used to help before they moved to England, and the parties had been some of her favorite memories. Marjory convinced Father to invite not only the orphanage children and the townschildren but also the Glen Eyrie servants, for many of them were far away from their families, too.

They sent handwritten invitations to all of the children, and, to the girls' surprise, Father knew the names of every single child they invited. Louisa and James Parker, Tristan Smith, Eleanor Dunby, and on and on it went. He had made a point to know each family in the town personally, and the impact it made was irreplaceable. Although, with the population boom in recent years, the girls knew he would not be able to remember them all forever.

A week before the party, Father ordered a 20-foot pine tree to be cut down in the nearby woods. The Palmer girls enlisted the help of Anna, Lanora, and Florenz to make hundreds of ornaments out of paper, wax, string, and clay.

The six of them spent one lazy afternoon trimming the tree, sipping wassail Cook had made, and dressing every mantelpiece and railing with fresh-cut pine boughs. They set up a tree in the servants' wing, too, and trimmed it with edible ornaments, such as popped corn and oranges. When they were finished, the house looked and smelled divine.

Dorothy felt a deep satisfaction in the preparations; Christmas was her favorite time of year, and she knew the children would feel loved and happy, even without a family of their own. The thought warmed her.

"Ah, I love Christmastime," Anna remarked and closed her eyes as she inhaled the scents of pine and orange.

Lanora looked around at the Palmer girls and remarked, "You would love Christmas in Crested Butte. The snow is so deep we have to wear skis to get around!"

"Truly?" Marjory said, wide-eyed.

"Yes, Miss Marjory," she continued. "The wealthy townspeople can hire one of Mister Thompson's four-horse sleighs, but the rest of us have to rely on our own two legs to get around."

"Lanora!" Anna hissed. "Do not be impertinent."

Lanora colored deeply and looked down.

"It is alright," Marjory said and placed a hand on her shoulder. "We did not take offense. The horse-drawn sleigh sounds lovely, but I think skiing sounds like even more fun."

Dorothy nodded her head and said, "We care deeply about all of you. Even you, Florenz." She poked him playfully with her elbow.

Now it was his turn to color. Dorothy did not notice, but Elsie saw a look in Florenz's eyes that she knew well. She had seen it also in Leo's eyes, the day she left England—one of longing, hope, desire.

Later that evening, as the Palmer girls and Father sat around the fire, they reminisced about Christmases past, some spent at Glen Eyrie but most spent at home in England with Mama. The girls took turns telling stories about the Christmas gifts they had received, and the tricks they had played on some of their more serious holiday house guests. This would be the first Christmas without Mama, and each one of them felt the loss very keenly. Father encouraged them to cherish the new memories they were making and to not let the pain of the past darken this wonderful season.

CHRISTMASTIME 1895
GLEN EYRIE

ON CHRISTMAS EVE MORNING, the day of the long-anticipated party, the girls awoke to a thick blanket of snow covering the ground. They worried the children might not be able to reach the house, but Father assured them he would send horse-drawn sleighs instead of carriages to pick them up. The servants bustled about the house making last-minute preparations, while delicious aromas wafted from the kitchen. Cook and her kitchen maids prepared a feast of creamed chicken, roast duck, and several kinds of potatoes. For dessert, they prepared fresh-made snow ice cream, pink and yellow lemonades, and spun sugars.

After breakfast, the girls spent several hours preparing the party favors: a crepe paper crown, candies, an orange, and a shiny new quarter for every child. They wrote little cards for the favors, with sayings like, "May you have a happy Christmas" and "We wish you the merriest of Christmases."

Elsie made a point to watch Dorothy's interactions with Florenz more closely during the party. *Did she feel the same for him?* she wondered.

The children began to arrive after lunch. The townschildren, Little Tommys and Georges, Maggies and Carolines, were dressed in their Sunday best. The children from the orphanage wore their usual outfits, but they appeared freshly starched; the workers had tied bows in the girls' hair and pinned flowers in the boys' lapels. The director of the orphanage and its workers had dolled up for the occasion, too, in fine muslin dresses and fancy up-dos.

The Glen Eyrie servants greeted the children and collected their coats and hats, then led them into the large sitting room that had been converted into a party room. The Palmer family, along with Lanora, Anna, Florenz, Jesse Bass, and Berty's family, clapped as they entered. When the children spied the pile of gifts under the tree, a few of them squealed and ran over to devour them. Father stepped in their path, turned them around, and assured them they would receive a gift in short order.

"He knows just what to do to diffuse a situation, does he not?"
Elsie whispered to Marjory, who nodded.

Father gave a short welcoming speech, after which Dorothy
organized games of musical chairs and hide-and-seek. Florenz taught
the children his favorite game: drop the handkerchief. He had the
children sit in a circle on the floor, then walked around behind them
and dropped a handkerchief in a chosen child's lap. The chosen child
then shot up and chased Florenz around the circle, in an attempt to
catch him before he returned to a sitting position.

Elsie glanced at Dorothy; she was watching Florenz with a smile on
her face. When Anna sidled up next to Dorothy, though, she looked
away from Florenz and focused her attention instead on Anna.

Perhaps she does not, Elsie thought.

The game-playing began to wind down just as suppertime
approached. The adults in the group herded the children into the Book
Hall, where several long tables had been set up, with a placard bearing
each child's name. They navigated the youngest children to their
assigned seats and took seats of their own.

While they ate, Father sat by the fireplace and told them the story of
Jesus Christ's birth and then read a few poems from the collection "A
Visit from St. Nicholas." The children's eyes glowed as Father
performed each character with a unique voice.

Marjory played the piano while Anna and Florenz led the party in
Christmas carols. From her seat in the back, Elsie observed as Dorothy
repeatedly gazed at Florenz during the performance. For a fleeting
second, she thought she saw a look of admiration on her face, but it
was gone as quickly as it came.

After the caroling, Marjory led the children to the 20-foot pine
Christmas tree in the corner of the hall. Their little eyes widened in
amazement at the gifts stacked neatly below. She played Santa Claus
and passed out a gift to each child; she could not help but notice the
stark contrast between the townschildren and the orphanage children.
The former ripped open the gift straight away, hardly pausing for a
moment; while the children from the orphanage lovingly clutched their

gifts, admiring the fine paper and caressing the soft silk bows. None of orphanage children unwrapped their presents that night, for they would be the only gift they received that Christmas. The thought made Marjory feel very grateful for the generosity of her Father and sisters.

A short time later, the children donned their coats and hats again and prepared to travel back to town. The Palmer girls stood at the doorway and kissed each child as they left. They watched them load into the sleighs and waved as they pulled away from the house, then they retreated back inside to sit a while by the crackling fire.

ON CHRISTMAS DAY, THE girls woke early before Father. He had given the servants the day off to enjoy the holiday with their families. Florenz's parents had been dead for some time, and he did not have any brothers or sisters, so Father invited him to spend the day with him and the girls.

In the kitchen, Elsie, Dorothy, and Marjory bustled about as they prepared a surprise Christmas breakfast for Father and Florenz. Dorothy had volunteered to cook. Everything had to be perfect.

"Alright. We have no servants, and no knowledge of cooking. But we are smart young ladies," Elsie said. "Besides, how hard can it be?"

Apparently, much harder than anticipated. "Here is an apron," Elsie said and handed it to Dorothy. "As you may."

Dorothy looked incredulous but then nodded in silent agreement.

"I know your secret," Elsie said and smiled at her sister.

"How—?" Dorothy began. "Oh, that Leo! He promised not to tell."

Back in England, on one of Leo's many visits, he had nipped below stairs to pinch an apple from the store cupboard. Instead, he had found Mrs. Broadbottom, the cook, and Dorothy standing at the stove. Mrs. Broadbottom was supervising Dorothy as she slowly stirred something in a large pot. He cleared his throat, and Dorothy had whipped around at the sound of it. Her eyes had widened as she had realized who it was.

When Leo told Elsie about it later, she did not believe him, but he convinced her to sneak downstairs to see for herself.

"Dorothy told me not to tell," he had confessed, "but I could not keep something this good to myself."

Now, in the Glen Eyrie kitchen, her sisters looked on in amazement as she whipped the eggs like a chef and rummaged in the cabinets to find an iron skillet. When breakfast was ready, Marjory went to wake Father while the other girls set the table in the dining room. Anna had been kind enough to light a fire for them, and the room felt cheerful and cozy.

Father stepped into the dining room and smiled widely at the display before him.

He took the first bite and said with his mouth full, "If Cook isn't careful, she will be out of a job!"

"Oh, Father! It is just a bit of eggs and bacon," Dorothy replied and blushed.

"It is wonderful, Dos."

The four of them sat down to enjoy the breakfast while the fire crackled merrily. Elsie poured a mug of coffee for each person, while Marjory fetched the gifts stacked up under the tree in the corner of the room. Each girl received one special gift from Father. For Elsie, a pair of white kid gloves she had been coveting since the first time she saw them in a haberdasher's window display in town. Dorothy opened a large, leather bound volume of maps—not just of Europe and America but New Zealand, Asia, Africa, and beyond. For Marjory, Father had bought the most beautiful porcelain doll she had ever seen, complete with silk parasol and genuine beadwork. Marjory was perhaps too old for dolls, but she adored it anyway.

Father gave Florenz a silver pocket watch with his initials engraved on the back. Dorothy smiled to herself, knowing Florenz preferred less-formal methods for telling the time. She and her sisters presented him with a new wool scarf and a cotton shirt.

The girls had pooled their money to purchase Father a handcrafted saddle bag to use on his long horse riding trips into the mountains. Jesse Bass had commissioned the work for them from a local leathersmith. Father felt overwhelmed by their generosity and rose to kiss his girls again. He felt as if his heart would burst with happiness. He had dreamed of this day for a long time—sitting around the fire at Glen Eyrie, opening gifts on Christmas day—but he never imagined it without his beloved Queen. It had been only a year since her death, but he knew she was with them even now, and he felt comforted by the thought.

Father picked up his Bible from the mantle and read the story of Christ's birth from the Book of Luke. His Quaker roots had taught him the importance of reflecting on the true reason for celebrating Christmas—a reverence his daughters emulated with grace. They held hands and bowed their heads as Father prayed for them, for the servants, for the residents of Colorado Springs, and, finally, for those without homes and loving families.

"Amen," he said and looked around at them, his heart full.

AFTER CHRISTMAS, THE WEATHER began to turn ugly. It snowed often and for several days in a row it was below zero degrees. During that time, Marjory fell ill. She was sick for what seemed like weeks. It started with a bad cold, which led into an infection in her lungs. Father sought treatment for her from every well-known physician in the area, but she would not recover. Then one night, the illness took a turn for the worst.

Elsie was awoken by a high-pitched, blood-curdling scream coming from Marjory's room. She sat bolt upright, reached for her dressing gown, and raced down the hallway. Dorothy had reached Marjory's room first. She stood in the doorway, wide-eyed in terrible fear.

As Elsie rounded the corner into her sister's room, she felt instantly sick at the sight before her. Marjory was sitting on her bed, dressed in her favorite white nightgown with delicate rosebuds around the collar. The entire front of her nightgown was drenched in blood. So were her hands and her mouth.

Elsie ran to her bedside and tried to lift up Marjory's nightgown, searching for a cut of some sort. Her mind could not process the obvious: her sister had coughed up all of that blood.

Marjory's hands shook as she pulled them away from her face. Her fear was reflected in Dorothy's eyes. She did not understand what was happening.

"Fetch Father, Dos," Elsie whispered, but Dorothy hung back and continued to stare into the room. "Now, Dos!" she screamed, which startled Marjory and made her begin to whimper.

The sound of her sister's cries jolted Dorothy out of her trance, and she ran to Father's room. She jostled him awake and urged him, "Come quickly, something is wrong!"

The servants called Dr. Jameson, who arrived within the hour. He did a thorough examination of poor Marjory. She was terribly weak from the loss of blood, but Elsie held her hand and wiped her brow with a cool cloth as the physician performed his exam.

At the end of it, Dr. Jameson rose from his place near her bed and asked to speak privately with Father. They left the room, and Dorothy and Elsie, with Anna's help, changed Marjory out of her spoiled nightgown and into a fresh one. As Marjory snuggled into bed and drifted off to sleep, Father returned and pulled them away. They descended the stairs to Father's den, where Dr. Jameson waited.

Elsie was the first to speak. "What is it, doctor? Will she be alright?"

Dr. Jameson appeared saddened by the news he was about to deliver. "Elsie, Dorothy, your sister has consumption."

Dorothy burst into tears then and clung to Father as Dr. Jameson continued on. "Do not be frightened by the dire reputation of the illness. It is painful and your sister will likely never be fully healthy again, but it is treatable. With the proper care and attention, she will pull through."

Elsie felt somewhat relieved and encouraged by this piece of information. She immediately began to consider the best course of action and also which servants would need to be trained in her sister's care.

Father felt deeply troubled. His heart could not bear another loss.

As they discussed Marjory's care, they began to hear servants bustling about and saw the sun rising through the curtains. Dorothy rose to check on Marjory, and Dr. Jameson prepared to leave.

"I will return this evening," he said, "to check on Miss Marjory and to train your servants."

OVER THE COURSE OF the next few weeks, things began to change for the residents of Glen Eyrie. Elsie had never seen Father so agitated and worried. She and Dorothy spent day and night at Marjory's bedside. Elsie would sit with Marjory while Dr. Jameson did his examinations, then after a few hours Dorothy would relieve her and read several chapters of a book to Marjory.

Marjory continued to cough up blood, and her breathing became very shallow and rasping. But after a month, her health improved, and it continued to do so as the weather grew warmer and she could spend more and more time outside.

The treatment for tuberculosis was simple, yet tricky. Patients needed to receive copious amounts of fresh air and sunshine, maintain a healthy diet, and avoid becoming over-excited. Father commissioned a glass porch to be built adjacent to her bedroom, where she could sit at peak hours and soak up these natural remedies. He altered the normal menu with Cook to add an abundance of fresh fruits and vegetables and wild-caught game.

Lanora and Anna kept Marjory's room as clean and tidy as possible, and they changed her sheets often. Father wanted her to be as comfortable as practicality would allow, so he insisted on these small adjustments to be observed by all. For months, Marjory was unable to ride her horse, take walks, or do much physical activity at all. She mostly stayed in her room. Luckily, her glass porch allowed her to be able to observe the comings and goings of her family members, visitors on the road, and wildlife that wandered onto the property.

Elsie often wondered how drastically different things would be if she or Dorothy had fallen ill. Marjory was an angel and easily pleased, so she embraced her illness as just a part of life. Elsie knew she would have had a much harder time accepting it, and Dorothy would have been downright depressed. On the other hand, if anyone deserved to be healthy and happy until the day they died, it was Marjory. Her illness felt unfair to everyone but her.

SUMMER 1896
GLEN EYRIE

BY THE END OF June, Marjory's health had improved greatly. She began to spend the warm summer afternoons taking short walks around the grounds—always with assistance from Lanora or one of her sisters, and often with a cane. She visited the Bertolottis at their cottage and even made a point to spend an hour or two here and there with Jesse and the other groomsmen. Jesse assured her the groomsmen were brushing her horse and riding him every chance they got, so he would be prepared for when his mistress was well enough to ride again. She brought them little chocolates as a thank-you for their kind attentions.

As Marjory improved, so did Father. The past few months, he had been living under a dark cloud of despair, but he had a spring in his step again. Elsie encouraged him to get back in the saddle, and he would spend hours riding. He scoured the hillsides for the prettiest wildflowers to place in Marjory's room. He even began entertaining guests again, once the threat of infection had passed, and he spent the occasional long afternoon at the Antlers or in the home of one of his old business friends.

Just as things around Glen Eyrie began to feel normal again, Elsie received a letter in the mail. It was from Leo.

My dearest, sweetest Elsie,

You must pardon me for neglecting to write sooner. I have been away much on business. You no doubt heard about my dear Father's passing. In March, I took over his business affairs, but I regret I am not as good at it as I would like.

You may wonder why I am writing to you now. I know you still receive the London papers, and I wanted to relay my good news first before you read it in the gossips. I am engaged, Elsie, since May.

You were always such a dear friend to me. I know you will be happy for me.

Your affectionate friend,
Leo

Elsie crumpled up the letter, tears streaming down her face, and threw it into the fire.

Part Two

Chapter Five

If I had a flower for every time I've thought of you ... I could walk
through my garden forever.
ALFRED LORD TENNYSON

1903
GLEN EYRIE

THE YEARS PASSED SLOWLY at first. Fall turned to winter, and winter
turned to spring, and, under the loving guidance of General Palmer and
his girls, Colorado Springs blossomed into a beautiful city. The
population had grown enormously since the girls' arrival eight years
before, and Father oversaw more expansions than he could count—
new roads, several parks (some well-manicured and others of natural
beauty), and schools.

Father experienced a major loss in his beloved hotel, the Antlers. It
burned to the ground in 1898. A courier arrived at the house, breathless

and harried, to deliver the news to poor Father. By the time he arrived on the scene, his years of work, his pride and joy, was ravaged by smoke and flame. All of the guests were accounted for, thank God, so he sat and watched until the hotel collapsed in on itself into a heap of ruin. The very next day, he called a meeting with his developers and contractors and discussed plans for the rebuild. He could not imagine Colorado Springs without the Antlers, and he knew he would never feel easy until it was up and running once more.

The rebuild became his main focus over the course of those next few years, and in 1901 it reopened to much fanfare and a completely full guest list. Owing in large part to Father's impeccable reputation among the elite, the Antlers once again became the major draw to the area.

After that, by selling his railroad companies and delegating many of his duties to his colleagues, Father effectively retired. His daughters thought they would never see the day, but, as expected, he was not "retired" for long. He threw himself into many new pursuits—or, rather, old pursuits made new—including exploring the area on horseback, entertaining friends at the hotel, and his new favorite: reviving Queen's dreams for Glen Eyrie.

Marjory, now 21, had become a refined, elegant, and strikingly beautiful young woman. She had a long, graceful neck, lithe limbs, and pure ivory skin. She had her mother's curly hair and expressive eyebrows but Father's pert nose and full lips. Her sisters knew she would not remain unmarried for long. She was too beautiful and too kind. But the tuberculosis, unfortunately, had altered Marjory's life forever.

On her "bad" days, she confined herself to her room, where she read, slept, and sat in her glass porch, watching the servants bustling about below. Most of the time, however, she felt almost like normal again; that is, until she pushed herself too far, which happened more often than Dr. Jameson would have liked. Under his care, she had learned how to cope with her debilitating illness. As for lessons in a cheerful outlook, she never needed any. Marjory was happy, carefree, sweet, and everyone's favorite.

At 22, Dorothy had become an advocate for the downtrodden, a voice for the voiceless. She cared little for socializing and even less for the pursuit of marriage. She decided long ago that only the deepest love would woo her to matrimony, and, so far, she had not found a single man she could tolerate for any length of time, let alone love. To his credit, Florenz had not given up on her, just as he promised. Dorothy could not conceive of losing his friendship and so never went so far as to have Father send him away. She carried on as if they were merely old friends.

Dorothy and Lanora were thick as thieves and spent much time together. Mama would have put a stop to their friendship long ago—or at least warned Dorothy not to become too close—but Father encouraged it. He saw nothing but good possibilities. Dorothy learned to relate to and love those of a different class, and Lanora benefitted from Dorothy's wisdom and education.

Dorothy kept up her visits to the local orphanage and constantly sought other ways to bolster the poor and lonely among them. She had inherited so much of Father's compassion. He took her along on his quarterly visits to the Colorado School for the Deaf and Blind. Father had donated the land to the institution a number of years ago, and now it had over 100 students. At first, Dorothy had been too afraid to converse with the children at the institution, for she did not know much about blindness nor deafness. She felt uneasy in their presence and unsure of herself, but, over time, the children's need for love and attention forced her to open her heart to them.

To Elsie, the past several years had positively flown by. Now 32, she had spent the whole of her twenties with no serious marriage proposals, no near-misses, nothing. Yes, she had met many eligible young men, but when it came down to it she could not imagine herself married to a single one of them. It did not help that they never offered anyway.

Elsie's extended singleness baffled everyone: Father, her sisters, her friends, and even the servants. Everybody knew Elsie had the world to

offer a man—she was beautiful, intelligent, accomplished, and wise—
yet no young man had offered her a permanent place in his heart and
his home. Father said they were blind idiots. As each year passed, Elsie
felt more forgotten and lonely, but she also felt determined to endure
this unexpected trial with grace and patience. And she did.

She had long since convinced herself to forget about the hope of a
future with Leo. His letter announcing his engagement was the nail in
the coffin. Elsie made a concerted effort to put him out of her mind,
and even if one of her sisters or Father enquired after his wellbeing, she
said, "He is doing well," and quickly changed the subject. She had not
told a soul about his last letter. It was a burden she bore alone.

Elsie became Father's partner in the massive remodel of Glen Eyrie.
Long ago, Queen had dreamed of a real castle—not wanting some
unsightly, modern home but rather turrets and climbing ivy and suits of
armor. Father said ever since the day Glen Eyrie was finished, she was
already plotting its remodel. Elsie loved their home, but the vision in
her head was as strong as an ocean tide. She and Father were similar in
that way.

Father commissioned the best stonemasons, architects, and workers
from miles around and put them to work. He brought in limestone
from Indiana, clay roof tiles from an old monastery in Europe, and
boulders from Bear Creek Valley, which the stonemasons cobbled
together to create the castle exterior.

Eventually, the remodel made it impractical for Father and the girls
to continue residing at Glen Eyrie, so they decided it was time to pack
up and move out for the duration of the project. Father took the girls
to Europe, where they scoured the old country for furniture, fireplaces,
and artwork to furnish the new Glen Eyrie. England and Scotland
yielded the largest bounty: a hammered metal fireplace plate, a full suit
of armor, and antique Chippendale chairs, among many other treasures.

As they collected the fine pieces, they had them sent to Colorado in
large crates. The girls adored being in England again, surrounded by
familiar sights and sounds and people. They visited all of their old
friends, apart from Leo. Elsie had told her sisters and Father that Leo

was abroad and unable to visit them—a lie, yes, but one she believed was completely necessary.

They took side trips to their former residences, and the girls brought small trinkets from back home in Colorado to present to the servants at Loseley Park, who were thrilled to see them again. Dorothy nearly jumped for joy that she had fulfilled her promise to return one day, if only for an afternoon.

The Palmers spent several months in London, where the girls were fitted for new dresses, and Father met with old business colleagues. On a bi-weekly basis, Father received large packets from the contractor back home. Elsie pressed him to see them—she was his partner for the remodel, after all—but he would not allow it. He wanted it to be a surprise.

The sea traveling, intense smog, and lack of sunshine made for a rather unpleasant trip for poor Marjory. Her body would not allow her to keep up with Father and her sisters; often, she would stay behind with Cecile while the others made their excursions. A weaker person would have been upset at missing out, but Marjory bore it with grace.

1903-1904
EUROPE

"MY! WELL, HELLO, MISS Palmers," a tall, handsome man said in surprise as he spotted the four Palmers enjoying tea at the historic Claridge's.

It was Lieutenant Richard Wellesley, the son of one of Mama's former friends. The girls had met him briefly back in the old days when they were still living in England. None of them had been impressed with him back then. Scrawny and pockmarked, they feared he would not survive basic training in the British Army.

The man who stood before them now appeared quite altered. He had grown a full four inches since they had last seen him, and, no longer the red-faced adolescent, he now sported a fine beard. He wore his uniform, which always made a man appear more manly. And Lieutenant Wellesley was quite a man.

"How wonderful it is to see you all. I had no idea you were back in town." The girls rose from their places at the table, and the lieutenant kissed their lace-gloved hands very lightly, lingering for a moment as he locked eyes with Marjory.

When they returned to their seats, Elsie let out a small cry as Dorothy's high-heeled boot made contact with her shin. Marjory giggled, which made her appear even more beautiful, and Father broke the silence with an "Ahem."

"Of course, General Palmer, I do apologize," he said and extended his hand. "I was ... distracted. It has been truly ages since I saw you last. It would have been, when, eighteen ninety-five?"

"Yes, I believe you are correct, Lieutenant Wellesley," Palmer said with a smile. "Your mother wrote to me when you became a lieutenant. I was very proud to hear the good news."

Wellesley colored slightly at the attention from the great General. "My small success in the British Army could never compare to your immense career, sir, but I do well for myself. And please, call me 'Wellesley.'"

Palmer nodded and motioned to the waiter to bring an extra chair. "Please, do join us." The waiter placed it exactly where Wellesley had hoped, next to Marjory. With a small smile, he nestled in next to her, looking quite pleased with himself.

For the next two hours, he regaled the party with stories of the army and his travels abroad during the Second Boer War. He had moved swiftly through the ranks and made quite a decent living for himself.

"How did you like South Africa, Wellesley?" Marjory asked. "Our aunt and uncle live there."

"It was very ... hot!" he replied with a laugh, and the girls laughed, too.

Last year he had met King Edward VII while at a special army event at Buckingham Palace. He described the king as tall and stern, with a face as cold as steel.

"I honestly would have rather met his mother," he said. "At least she might have been kinder."

Marjory's face lit up at the mention of Queen Victoria, for she admired her more than anyone on God's green earth. In fact, Elsie remembered that she had mourned her death for a solid two months after it happened.

"No queen will ever be as graceful and eloquent and wise as she!" she had moaned and cried into the crook of her elbow upon hearing the news.

They had tried to convince her not to wear her mourning clothes, but she would not be persuaded. She had come down to breakfast the next day in full regalia—black gown, black gloves, and even a black lace veil, to hide her tears.

The sound of her sister's voice interrupted Elsie's memory.

"We had a large party for the Queen's Diamond Jubilee," Marjory was saying.

"Did you?" the lieutenant replied.

"We did," she said. "It was the event of the year. Dorothy and I painted old bed sheets with the English flag, and our cook made tea, scones, and cucumber sandwiches. Father rang a bell and led us in a prayer for Her Royal Highness's continued health and the prosperity of England. Several of the servants joined in," she continued. "The ones who have English sympathies, of course."

"Of course," Wellesley stated.

"It was truly magical. It made my sisters and I miss England very much."

Wellesley perked up and asked, "Will you, perhaps, return to England to live one day?"

"I do not know what the future holds for me," Marjory replied, "but I do love this country and would be very happy to return."

Wellesley stared at Marjory and smiled. "Well, I am due at my mother's house very soon," he said as he stood to leave. "I have so enjoyed our chance encounter." He directed this at Marjory. "Will you still be in town tomorrow?"

"We will be here tomorrow, yes," Palmer replied, noticing his concentrated attention on Marjory. "Would you care to join us for tea again?"

Wellesley looked very pleased. "I would, indeed. Very much. Until tomorrow, then."

He shook hands with the party and lingered again with Marjory's hand very near his lips. She colored slightly and watched him leave.

The next day, they met Wellesley for tea, as planned. This time, he wore not his uniform but a fine grey suit cut perfectly to emphasis his broad shoulders. All three of the Palmer girls felt quite swoony at the sight of him—even Dorothy—but none more so than Marjory.

The party chatted pleasantly for two hours, and at the end Wellesley pulled Palmer aside. "If I may speak with you in private, sir, for a brief moment."

"Of course."

"Sir … General Palmer … I would greatly appreciate your permission to write to your youngest daughter, Miss Marjory," he said, confidently.

"That would be most welcome, Wellesley," he replied, impressed with the man's directness. "Thank you for your courtesy. Most men these days overlook the simple but most appreciated gesture of asking a father's permission. You have mine."

He looked immensely pleased at Palmer's reply and rushed off to Marjory's side. She stood and he whispered into her ear as her sisters looked on. Excited, she began to cough and sat back down quickly.

"Oh, our sister has—" Dorothy began but received another swift kick to the shin. She looked at the source of the kick, and Marjory shook her head slightly.

For fear Lieutenant Wellesley would catch on, Marjory quickly wrote something on a small slip of paper. Their postal address in Colorado, no doubt.

Wellesley bid farewell to the party again, wished them *bon voyage* for the duration of their trip abroad, and promised Marjory he would post a letter that very evening. That way she would have one to read upon her return to Colorado. How very thoughtful.

Later, after he had left, Dorothy rounded on Marjory. "Why did you have to kick me?"

"Dos. I do not want the lieutenant to know anything about my condition. He sees me as lively and vivacious, and I do not want to ruin that."

"Whatever you say," Dorothy replied.

MARJORY WAS IN HIGH spirits the whole rest of the trip. Wellesley's promise to send his first letter to Colorado was kind but felt like torture to Marjory. How could she wait another six weeks to read it?

The Palmers stayed in London a few days more. While Elsie and Marjory visited friends and toured their old haunts in town, Dorothy and Father visited one of the many workhouses in London. Throughout their time in Europe, Dorothy had talked incessantly about making a visit, but Father had said the workhouses were no place for a young woman. Dorothy begged him until he finally relented.

"You will not easily forget what you are about to see," Father said somberly as he led her in.

Dorothy knew the conditions in the workhouses were subpar, but she was appalled at the lack of windows, poor air quality, and sheer number of workers standing so close together their elbows touched. As she moved down the aisle, she spied a few women sleeping under the tables.

Father followed her gaze and bent down to whisper in her ear, "These women are exhausted. They are made to work fourteen hours a day—and sometimes as many as eighteen hours—with very little time to rest. See," he said and pointed to a pair of workers. "A mother and child are working side-by-side."

"Why—?"

"Why do the foremen employ children? It is acceptable under the law, but I find it atrocious."

"That little one there looks no more than four years old," Dorothy said, shocked. She wiped away a tear that had trickled down her face. "I think I have seen enough."

Out on the pavement, Father held Dorothy as she sobbed into his chest. "There, there," he said and patted her hair. "Now, let us see the good that can come from this."

Their carriage jostled them across town, eventually stopping in front of a large brick house. As Dorothy stepped out, she could hear children laughing as they played nearby. She turned to smile at Father.

"This is a children's home run by an old friend of mine, from the war."

A large man threw open the door at the sight of the stopped carriage and bellowed, "General!"

The two men embraced, and the large man hugged Father around the neck. "You are very welcome! And this must be Dorothy," he said and stuck out his hand.

"Yes, I am," she said awkwardly.

"You are most welcome, too," he said and smiled at her. They followed him up the stairs and into a large foyer.

"Tell me, Mason, how is it going?" Father asked.

"It has not been easy since we lost Ruth, but we do our best."

As Father and Mason talked about the state of the home and reminisced about Ruth and the old days, Dorothy explored the grand house. The parlor and sitting room had been converted into classrooms, and she peeked in through one of the doors to see several children staring with rapt attention as the teacher led them in Latin lessons. She returned to Father's side.

"Who are these children?" Dorothy asked. "Are they orphans?"

"Some are, yes," Mason explained. "Others we rescued from the workhouses. Their parents owed a debt and sent them to work, but we could not leave them there. Ruth and I believed all children deserve a childhood, so we opened our home—at first to one child and then to ten, and now we have thirty-seven children. We hope and pray to find loving homes for the orphans; as for the workhouse children, we pay as much of their parents' debts as possible and give them a place to stay until their parents work off the rest."

"This is brilliant, truly," Dorothy said. "I cannot fathom how any parent could send their child to a workhouse. And worse, many of the parents have no choice; they are working alongside their children. You are doing a wonderful thing, Mister Mason."

"That is high praise coming from a young woman such as yourself," Mason replied.

"Why do you say so, sir?" Dorothy said.

"You are a woman of birth and status. Many of your kind either cannot or will not expose themselves to the harsher realities of our world. Yet here you are. You are a compassionate young women, Miss Dorothy, and I commend you for it."

Dorothy blushed slightly and Father reached out to take her hand. As he led her to the carriage outside, he bent down and whispered in her ear, "I am so proud of you."

1904
GLEN EYRIE

WHEN THE TIME FINALLY came to head back to Glen Eyrie, the girls felt very much as if they were returning home. They had loved visiting Europe and spending so much time in their beloved spots, but Colorado was home to them now.

Jesse Bass and several other grooms met their train at the station and conveyed them to Glen Eyrie. When they rounded the bend toward the house, the four of them were shocked to see how much progress had been made. It was nearly finished.

The house had always been grand and beautiful, but now before them stood the most magnificent castle they had ever laid eyes on. It looked as if it had existed in the valley for hundreds of years.

Everything about it had been done with the utmost care and attention to detail. Father felt as if he had been transported back to his honeymoon and gazed upon one of the ancient castles he and Queen loved so much. He knew she would be beaming with pride if she could see it now.

With the contractor's supervision, Father had secretly planned numerous modern improvements, including inventions the girls had never seen before.

"So *this* is what was in the packets!" Elsie said as Father modeled the cutting-edge fire prevention system.

He had also developed a groundbreaking flue system that led chimney smoke out of the house and into the atmosphere above, electrical lights throughout, and a pasteurization plant for Marjory's consumption.

Father would often say Louis Pasteur was one of the most interesting men he had ever met. And he had met a lot of interesting men. After Marjory fell ill, Father was desperate to find a cure. He read about the link between consumption and unpasteurized milk and decided to travel to Paris to meet the author of the study. By the end of his visit, Father had convinced Mr. Pasteur to allow him to take a small plant back to Colorado with him. That was several years ago, but he finally had it installed and in working order.

The servants were very happy to have the Palmers in residence once again. Their return signaled the end of almost two years of renovations; no more sawing, hammering, chiseling, or the like.

Later, in Elsie's quarters, Dorothy and Marjory sat on her bed when they heard a light rap on the door. "Who is it?" she called.

"It is us!" a girl's voice replied, almost in a whisper.

Elsie glanced at her sisters, who grinned back at her. "Come in!"

Barreling through the door came Lanora, Anna, and Florenz, the latter of which looked quite handsome in a new, fashionable hairstyle. Elsie stole a quick glance at Dorothy. She had not seen Florenz in ages—had they written? Had she missed him at all? Elsie could not tell.

They passed out gifts to each of their friends—a silk-edged

nightgown for Anna, a beautifully carved antique jewelry box for Lanora, and an ivory-handled pocket knife for Florenz.

"We have a few surprises of our own!" Lanora exclaimed. "Missus Simmons has been training Anna to be a housekeeper, and I have been declared a right and proper housemaid!"

"That is wonderful news!" Elsie replied. She left out that Father had informed them of these changes months ago; Mrs. Simmons had written to Father while they were away, seeking his permission.

"And I have been showing Anna how to track the eagles," Florenz said. "We venture out once a week and make notes on their habits."

"Fascinating creatures," Anna said and blushed.

Dorothy looked up at Florenz, who wore an odd expression. She smiled at him, and he smiled back.

ONCE THEY HAD SETTLED back into life in Colorado, inspired by what she had learned while in England, Dorothy began to spend most of her time at the orphanage and the Colorado School for the Deaf and Blind—preparing meals, mentoring the children, and assisting them with schoolwork.

Visiting the children, learning about their lives, and being able to make a concerted effort to better their situations set her heart on fire. The more she volunteered, the more she wanted to volunteer, and after a particularly grueling week in which she spent nearly 50 hours away from home, Father asked for a private interview with her after dinner one evening.

"Darling," he began, "I am worried about you."

"You do not need—" she began.

"Of course I do, Dos," he cut across her. "It is a wonderful thing you are doing by visiting the orphanage and the school as often as you do, but you need to look after yourself, as well."

Dorothy paused to collect her thoughts, then responded, "Elsie and Marjory's endless chatter about their friends and their shopping trips and the remodel of the castle are exhausting to me, Father," she confessed. "My eyes have been opened, and I cannot see the importance of trivialities any longer."

Father pondered this for a moment before replying. "Be careful you do not live too long in that world, darling, or you will end up with a bitter heart instead of a soft one."

He squeezed her shoulder as he stepped past her and left her to her thoughts.

Chapter Six

We should a guest love while he loves to stay, and when he likes not,
give him loving way.
ENTRANCE TO GLEN EYRIE

SPRING & SUMMER 1904
GLEN EYRIE

SINCE THE COMPLETION OF the remodel, Glen Eyrie had become
quite the tourist attraction. Father and the girls did not mind; in fact,
they were immensely proud of the castle and believed it should be
enjoyed by all. On weekends, Berty opened the front gate to allow
visitors to pass through. Many of them would bring picnic baskets and
enjoy a meal by the stream. Others—the brave ones—would approach
the castle and ask for an interview with Palmer. Being the gracious man
that he was, he never refused anyone.

Often the girls would find Father giving a guided tour of each room, regaling the crowd on the many modern improvements he had made. The crowd would give Father great satisfaction by gasping and *ahh*-ing when appropriate. He would always end his tour in the Book Hall, his pride and joy, a long room with cathedral ceilings, enormous windows, a fireplace standing 15 feet tall and nearly as wide, and Elsie's John Singer Sargent portrait. The far wall was lined with glass-front bookshelves, with a choir loft above boasting an open fretwork railing and enough seats for 20 people. Big game heads were mounted on the walls, and an elegant chandelier hung above a tufted leather couch.

Below the Book Hall was Father's private bowling alley, the first of its kind in Colorado. This was of particular interest to the men who came to visit.

The Glen Eyrie remodel was the talk of the town. Newspapermen came from Denver and beyond to take photographs of the castle, with Father standing proudly out front. Not a day went by when they did not have at least five visitors, and the Palmers took it all in stride. The news of the remodel had reached the ears of their family and friends across the country and in Europe, and many of them wrote letters announcing their intentions to come for an extended stay that summer or the next.

One of the first to come for a visit was their close friend from back in England, Lady Caroline Hollister. She had written to ask for a visit to their "famous" home, and the girls could not resist her—she was a whirlwind of fun, jokes, laughter, and all-around good-naturedness.

Upon hearing the news of Caroline's planned trip, Dorothy sighed and said, "Let us hope this visitor is better than the last. I will never forget the infamous Dottie trip."

Two years before, during a brief family trip to England, they invited their old friend Dorothy Comyns-Carr, "Dottie," for a long visit. She had agreed wholeheartedly and spent 10 months with the Palmers in Colorado.

"Oh, Dos, she was fine," Elsie replied.

"She hated it here, remember? She hated the snow and the wind and the rattlesnakes, and nothing could compare to England. She even hated President Roosevelt!"

Father began to laugh at this. "I think she took my dislike of his policies to heart, poor girl," he said and shook his head.

"Well, she liked it here in the end," Marjory remarked.

"After months spent here, she finally liked it a little bit. My, what high praise."

"Caroline will be different," Elsie insisted.

When Lady Caroline Hollister arrived at the Denver and Rio Grande Depot, Father and the girls greeted her on the platform with flowers. The moment her feet hit the ground, she ran to the girls, threw her arms around them, and wrapped them up in a big bear hug. She stuck out her hand to shake Father's, but he pulled her into a hug instead. Caroline went on and on about the spectacular views and the booming city of Colorado Springs, how taken she was with it all, and how excited she was to finally be there. She was smitten with Pike's Peak, adored the wild animals near the road, and was generally pleased by all that she surveyed.

Elsie smiled smugly at Dorothy as Caroline said, "This is entirely more marvelous than you let on, Elsie! And the photographs you sent must have been taken ten years ago!"

"I assure you they were taken not one year ago, but that proves how much the city has changed and grown in only a year's time." She patted Father's arm.

On the ride to Glen Eyrie, Caroline talked animatedly about her journey by rails. She asked Father many questions about the railway and the path it cut across mountains, rivers, and plains of endless tall grass. Father adored the attention and told her stories of the railroad wars, the land grabs, and the greedy businessmen he had encountered during his years as a railroad man.

During one particularly exciting story, Caroline looked across at Elsie and winked. Elsie smiled back and mouthed, "Thank you."

As they rounded the bend into the Valley of the Eagle's Nest, Caroline declared it a "most wondrous sight to behold." She marveled at Major Domo and caught a glimpse of the eagle in its nest, with three little babies. They left the carriage and horses with Jesse Bass and continued on foot up to the main house.

Caroline was absolutely struck by the stone castle, with its turret and gables and leaded glass windows. It reminded her very much of the castles in England and Scotland, but she had never before seen such an exact replica here in America. Everything had been done to perfection, exactly the way she would have designed it had she been the owner. Caroline could not conceive that it had only been completed just a few months prior, for it had the appearance of a great old age.

"It reminds me of the Biltmore Estate!" she declared.

"No, indeed," Father replied, embarrassed.

"Truly! A couple years past, my father had business with Mister Biltmore, and he was gracious enough to allow us to stay at his magnificent home. If it can even be called a home. It is, in essence, a palace. The Biltmore Estate is vastly beautiful. But this ..." she paused. "This is idyllic," she said and Father smiled.

As they walked up the brick path to the front door, Berty and Mrs. Simmons were there to receive Caroline and remove her hat and parasol. As she glanced about the entrance hall and subsequent parlor and dining room, she spied rich oriental rugs and rare oil paintings, along with photographs of Father's family and several of Queen.

"Mister Palmer, your late wife was a real beauty. I miss her very much," she said, sad but for a moment.

"Thank you, my dear Caroline, we miss her, too."

Elsie and Mrs. Simmons showed her to her quarters on the second floor. Typically, guests stayed on the third floor—it provided privacy for both guests and residents—but Elsie had insisted Caroline room near her and her sisters instead. Mrs. Simmons acquiesced and had the room done up with every luxury a guest would enjoy. She swung open the door to reveal a large, bright room with windows facing west and cheerful, floral-printed furnishings. Caroline admired the fireplace in the corner, which had unusual-looking tiles.

Elsie noted her friend's furrowed brow and followed her gaze. "A creation of Father's dear friends, Mister and Missus Van Briggle," Elsie explained.

"Van Briggle? Yes, I have heard of them. I saw an exhibition of their work once in Paris. Art Nouveau or some such thing."

"Did you?" Elsie exclaimed. "They are a favorite in this household."

"You best wash the train off yeh and come down in an hour for supper," Mrs. Simmons said to Caroline and motioned to Elsie to leave her.

Elsie winked at her friend and closed the door behind her.

DURING CAROLINE'S STAY, EVERY day was filled with activities and exploring. Elsie, Dorothy, and Caroline toured the city by carriage and on horseback, spent hours roaming the grounds of Glen Eyrie, took tea at the Antlers several times per week, and went on hikes to Dorothy Falls and the Garden of the Gods. On days when she felt strong enough, Marjory came along, too.

Occasionally, Father allowed Florenz to accompany the girls on their little trips. He was not a skilled horseman, but he acted as chaperone in Father's absence. He and Dorothy were still thick as thieves, a fact Caroline noticed immediately and teased Dorothy about in private. Even though Elsie was convinced the pair of them would be married, Caroline was not so sure. Clearly, Florenz was in love with Dorothy. But was Dorothy in love with Florenz? She was not certain.

In the evenings, after supper, they played cards by the fire and took turns reading aloud. Marjory played piano and sang.

During one particular evening, Elsie unwrapped a bundle of letters she had saved over her years of correspondence with Caroline. As she read a few aloud, the girls sputtered and laughed at the retelling of Caroline's adventures among the upper crust of London society.

"Did Missus Bloomsbury *really* wear nothing but her knickers to the opera?" Elsie snorted with laughter.

"She did! At least, she tried!" Caroline exclaimed.

"What was she protesting?" Dorothy asked. "Public decency?"

"Not quite. She is a suffragette. But why she chose the opera to make a statement about women's votes is quite beyond me."

"Perhaps she liked the idea of a captive audience," Dorothy replied, and the girls burst into laughter once again.

The girls could easily relate to Caroline and her way of straddling the divide between being high-born and feeling uneasy around snobbish people, for they experienced the same almost daily. They had been born into a life of luxury, but they felt very much like ordinary young women. In her younger years, Elsie had cared very much about impressing the right people in society, but age and experience had made her wiser. Now she knew it was a fruitless endeavor to attempt to please high-brow people, for they had a nasty habit of being consistently disappointed. Even Father, who liked and approved of nearly everyone, enjoyed Caroline's anecdotes and shook with laughter.

After Father went to bed, the girls begged Caroline to tell them all about her fiancé, Charles, and her wicked future mother-in-law.

"She is as mean as they come, I tell you. On my wedding night I truly believe she will come into our room and try to put a pillow over my face," Caroline exclaimed to gasps of shock from the Palmer girls. "I tell you the truth! Never a meaner woman lived."

"Why marry him?" Marjory asked, innocently.

Caroline thought for a moment before replying, "Because despite his dragon of a mother—"

Dorothy and Marjory chuckled at this.

"Despite that," Caroline continued, "I love him. Charles is a good man. And he loves me so dreadfully much. I could not bear to see him heartbroken."

Florenz made a loud grunt from his spot on the sofa.

"What?" Caroline asked. "Do you think me vain?"

"No," Florenz replied. "It is just that—" he paused.

"Go on."

"You should not marry a man for fear of breaking his heart. You claim to love him. But if you truly loved him, you would not say such things."

Caroline pondered this. "Do you believe, then, that each partner must love the other in equal amounts? Are not many marriages built on one partner's love and the other's politeness?"

"You shock me!" Dorothy declared.

"I am just being practical. Yes, I love him. But he loves me much more, it is true. Should I not marry him and hope my love will increase?"

"Surely not!" Florenz said. "If you cannot say in good faith that you love him as much as he loves you, I beg you, put him out of his misery." He looked at Dorothy, then stood up and left the room.

Elsie glanced at her sister, but she avoided her gaze.

Later that evening, from her bedroom window, Elsie saw Dorothy and Florenz on the patio below. She could not hear their voices and did not dare open the window for fear of making herself known to them. She watched as Florenz paced around, gesturing animatedly, then walked right up to her sister and kissed her. Dorothy seemed stunned but then pushed him away, her hand on his chest. Florenz stormed off and Dorothy stared after him for a moment, then followed him out of sight of Elsie's window.

Elsie continued to look out the window for a few moments, then climbed into bed and tucked the covers up under her chin.

ON A FINE, CLEAR day in mid-June, Elsie took Caroline on a trip up Pike's Peak on the cog railway, a steam locomotive that carried passengers up the steep climb to the summit of the mountain. They spied many varieties of wildlife through the train windows, including one in particular Caroline had never seen before.

"Is that a mountain lion!" she exclaimed and recoiled in her seat.

Elsie patted her knee and said, "Yes, dear, but it cannot come through the glass." She turned her head away and chuckled softly.

"I see you laughing at me, Elsie Palmer!" her friend said in mock disgust.

At the summit, the pair disembarked from the train and stood at the edge of the west-facing overlook, taking in the 360-degree views of the mountain ranges stretching as far as the eye could see.

"'For purple mountain majesties,' Miss Bates wrote. I always wondered why she had described them as 'purple.' But now I see. They really do look purple from up here," Caroline remarked. "You are so lucky to live here."

Elsie smiled and said, "Father met Miss Bates a few times, did you know that?"

"Indeed? How marvelous."

"Yes. She came in the eighteen-nineties to teach an English course at Father's college. He put her up in the Antlers. Can you imagine, she and her friends came up here on wagons and mules!"

"Sounds … uncomfortable," Caroline replied and winked. Elsie burst into laughter.

THROUGHOUT THE HOT SUMMER months, Elsie and Dorothy, and sometimes Father and Marjory, took Caroline into the areas around Colorado Springs. She especially enjoyed taking the waters at Manitou Springs. Elsie absolutely detested the taste and smell of the natural mineral water, but Caroline adored it for its supposed healing properties.

They took her north to Denver, where they visited the State Capitol and spent many lazy hours at Washington Park. They rented bicycles and pedaled around the lakes, admiring the paddle boats filled with lovers.

Caroline was fascinated by the rich and vibrant history of these Front Range towns, but she longed to explore the wild, untouched beauty of the Rocky Mountains. Father insisted they travel only on the routes he had developed and organized use of his old private car, the Nomad. They traveled in style to the Great Sand Dunes and the Black Canyon of the Gunnison, but Elsie wanted to take her somewhere special: Ouray.

Elsie had never been there herself, but Father loved the little town
and talked about it all the time. Ouray was named for Chief Ouray of
the Uncompaghre Ute Indians. He was a brave man who once traveled
to Washington, D.C., to attempt to negotiate a treaty on behalf of his
tribe. Father admired Chief Ouray's boldness and had made certain to
bring the Denver and Rio Grande to the little town, to bolster its
economy and to provide easy access for his many trips.

The train ride to Ouray took nearly an entire day, but the scenery
was positively unparalleled. Southern Colorado was completely
different than the north—steeper mountains, rockier cliffs, fewer trees,
and an overwhelming sense of grandeur.

The train arrived at Ouray's quaint train station, and, as they
disembarked, the girls could not believe their eyes. Nestled between
enormous, jagged cliffs lay a small town that looked like something out
of a storybook about the Swiss Alps. For a moment, Elsie thought she
had been transported back in time to her and Father's trip to
Switzerland. Many of the homes and businesses had charming
gingerbread-style roofs and woodwork, and they could hear the faint
rumble of the nearby waterfalls.

That first afternoon, they toured the famous Box Canyon Falls, a
waterfall encased in an intricate series of open-air ravines and caves.
Within the caves, they had to walk along a wooden bridge that hugged
the rock walls—it was all rather thrilling, especially in high boots and
dresses.

They sampled the town's rich fare, including the best saltwater taffy
they had ever tasted, and lodged at the Beaumont Hotel, a quaint but
elegant hotel at one end of town. Caroline noted that the hotel was a
perfect contrast between the rugged beauty of the Wild West and the
charm of old Europe.

WHILE THE PALMERS AND Caroline were away on their tour of the
mountains, Mrs. Simmons put the entire servant staff to work. The

female servants spring-cleaned the castle from top to bottom, while the male servants tended to the outside of the castle—trimming trees, cleaning rain gutters, and tending to other once-per-year chores.

When Palmer was away, Berty and Mrs. Simmons allowed a certain amount of freedom. It was not uncommon to find a maid reading a novel in the choir loft, or the grooms playing a round or two in Palmer's bowling alley. They did not fear being found out, for Palmer had given his permission for such activities long before the trip took place.

Many of the servants had worked before in houses much like Glen Eyrie—large, owned by a wealthy master—but none had experienced the same level of kindness of the Family. Palmer approached the running of his household the same way he approached his business deals: with fairness and grace. It made a lasting impression on everyone who stepped foot inside Glen Eyrie.

Chapter Seven

Whatever our souls are made of, his and mine are the same.
EMILY BRONTË

1905
GLEN EYRIE

AFTER A PERIOD OF many months, and to the Palmer girls' sadness, Caroline returned home to England. When she was gone, life quickly returned to its normal pace. Elsie and Marjory entertained friends, Dorothy continued her volunteer work in town, and the three of them went on innumerable horse rides with Father. Everyone missed Caroline's contagious exuberance, but Elsie felt her loss most keenly of all. She became listless and bored, eager for another adventure yet without any prospect of one. In truth, she was lonely.

Elsie began to believe that she had quite lost her bloom. Years of unfulfilled dreams had taken their toll, especially on the dark circles under her eyes. The castle remodel and Caroline's subsequent visit had been good distractions, but with a long future stretched out before her and no knowledge of what it would hold, she was bombarded by the perceived terribleness of her situation. No one had ever called her a spinster, or even hinted at the horrible word, but nevertheless she felt the sting of being a maiden. Her sisters had yet to marry, but even so, she felt isolated in her grief.

Marjory could sense her older sister's pain and often tried to encourage her with little praises or notes of appreciation, but no amount of niceties could quell the emptiness in Elsie's heart. It ran deep down to the most hidden places of her heart—where only time spent in prayer could reach. She smiled and appeared happy and never let any of her friends see her in anguish, but late at night she would lie awake in the dark and beg God for relief.

Sometimes she wished she could be more like Dorothy—perfectly content to be unmarried and, at least outwardly, completely confident. On occasion, Elsie's admiration for her sister's contentment turned into resentment, which drove her to do and say things she would not otherwise do nor say. Florenz and Dorothy's close bond reminded her of her long-lost friendship with Leo Myers. She could not bear the thought of Leo, happily married with probably one or two children by now, while she was still waiting, endlessly.

When her grief became too much, Elsie would lock herself in her room for a day or two, lost in her own head. Sometimes, Dorothy would attempt to coax her out, with promises of entertainment, but, without fail, her attempts resulted in the silent treatment until Elsie had enough time to talk herself down.

Talking herself down was a practice she had developed with assistance from Father, who recognized in his oldest daughter a tendency to become defensive and overwhelmed when the reality of her situation became too much to handle. Father prayed often for a happy marriage for Elsie, and she cherished those prayers more than she could ever convey.

DOROTHY BURST INTO THE library, red-faced and short of breath. She had just returned from a walk with Florenz. The pair of them usually walked for an hour or more in the evenings, but she had only been gone for 10 minutes. Elsie was the first to notice her younger sister's altered appearance.

"What is it, Dos? What's wrong?" she asked her.

"Oh dear," she moaned. "Oh dear, what will I do?" She paced the room and wrung her hands. She reached up to grab hold of a large vase from the fireplace mantel, but Father quickly grabbed it from her before she could smash it on the floor.

"Child!" He pinned her arms to her sides. "Calm yourself, my darling!"

Dorothy had a look of fury in her bright eyes, one Elsie had never seen before in her life. "Sit down, Dos," she said, "and tell us what happened."

Dorothy paused a moment to catch her breath and then said, "He wanted to go for a walk before turning in for the night. We often take walks after dinner, you know. But this time was different."

"Different how?" Marjory asked.

"He has tried to kiss me many times in the past, but this time when he leaned in towards me, he bent down on one knee instead."

"Oh!" Elsie let out a small shriek.

"Oh, Father," Dorothy moaned. "He had a ring and everything. He told me he had been planning that moment for the past several years. Years, Father!"

Father wrapped his strong arms around his middle child and brushed her hair with his hands. Her reaction to a man's proposal may have seemed bizarre to outsiders, but he understood his daughter's fear. She was destined for a different kind of life, and marrying a common house boy was not part of it.

Elsie could not listen to any more. She fled the room with a swish of her skirt, climbed the staircase two-by-two, and mounted the second-floor landing. When she reached her bedroom, she slammed the door behind her and sunk onto the bed. Only then did she let out a loud sob and allow the tears to fall.

After an hour or so, Dorothy and Marjory quietly crept into their sister's room and gently closed the door behind them.

"Elsie," Marjory said and walked softly to where she lay stretched across her bed. "Elsie, it's us."

"Please leave me be," she replied in muffled tones. "I am fine, I just want to be alone."

Marjory pulled away, but Dorothy advanced to her sister's side. "I know you are upset, Els. And I am sorry. I know you admire Flor—"

"How can you be so dense, Dos?" Elsie cut across her. "It is not Florenz I am crying about! It is the fact that you receive a proposal from a man who says he has loved you for years, and you find that utterly disturbing. And I, who have been preparing and readying myself for marriage since I was a girl, have had none! I am utterly forgotten. It is hopeless."

"Do not say that, Elsie," Marjory said and hugged her. "You have been faithful in waiting for the right man all these years. You have not wavered, you have not settled, and God will bless with you a happy marriage in His timing and not before."

"I used to think that was true," Elsie sniffled. "But I am beginning to wonder if I have been made a fool. Perhaps I should have taken a different path, not been so choosy."

"Trust me," Marjory said. "It will happen. You will see."

DESPITE HER SISTERS' ENCOURAGEMENT, Elsie remained in a dark mood for several weeks. Father attempted to cheer her up by inviting her closest friends to the house and promising her a lovely trip to the mountains, but she was unmoved.

"I know what she needs, Father," Marjory said as she entered his den. He was nose-deep in something Dickens.

"I'm listening."

"She needs Mama ... or rather, someone like her."

Father looked confused, but then it dawned on him: Lottie.

Marjory felt pleased by Father's eagerness to bolster his eldest daughter's happiness. That was his way—unfailingly kind.

"You are brilliant, my darling, absolutely brilliant. The president of the college asked me only last week to make a recommendation for a new curator for a museum they hope to build. William's expertise in museum curation will be the perfect fit."

Father wrote to Aunt Lottie and her husband, William Sclater, right then and there, and had the butler post the letter for the evening collection. The Sclaters lived in South Africa, so they had to wait six weeks for a reply, but when it came, Elsie jumped for joy. Lottie and William would return to Colorado!

It took some months to wrap up William's duties in South Africa and to prepare to make the move stateside. They decided to travel by land for part of the way, through Zanzibar and down the Nile. William, an avid bird-watcher, photographed their journey, which became a lasting tribute to an epic adventure.

In July, Father received a telegram from the Sclaters. They were in New York City and would arrive to Colorado in six days' time. Elsie could barely contain her excitement.

Aunt Lottie had not always been a favorite among the Palmer girls. There was a time when the girls felt only resentment towards their young aunt. One of Mama's much-younger siblings, she had grown up with Palmer as a Father figure, even calling him "Uncle," and had spent many happy childhood years at Glen Eyrie. But she eventually won them over with her gay spirit and unquenchable thirst for fun.

Why she married a stuffy museum curator, no one would ever understand, but somehow their relationship worked beautifully.

Elsie looked up to Aunt Lottie and admired her tenacity. Last time they had seen her was in 1902 in London. She and William had traveled there from South Africa so Aunt Lottie could receive an award from the King of the Royal Red Cross. During the Boer War, she had organized a massive operation to provide comfort packets for the troops, and finally, over 20 years later, she was recognized for her efforts.

It was an incredible awards ceremony, and they had celebrated and rejoiced for hours. After that, she had accompanied the Palmers on their return voyage to America. While in New York City, they had visited Lottie's brothers, Nathan and Chase, whom she had not seen in years. The group had toured the city, taken in a few shows, and after a few days' time, boarded the Nomad to head to Colorado.

She could only spend a month at Glen Eyrie, but what a month it had been! Parties and picnics and spontaneous rides into the mountains. Lottie had relished being back home again, and Father absolutely adored having her there, for she was just as big an enthusiast for outdoor activities as he was.

Now, four years later, it would be no different.

Marjory spotted Aunt Lottie waving out the window of the train car and waved back animatedly. When they disembarked from the train, Aunt Lottie threw her arms around all four Palmers at once.

"I cannot believe I am home again!" she exclaimed. "It feels like forever, believe me. South Africa is not pleasant this time of year."

William stepped out of the train car behind her and approached Palmer with an outstretched hand. Father shook his hand at first but then pulled him into an embrace.

"I am so terribly glad you are here, dear William. The college is lucky to have you," Father said and clapped him on the back.

"We are thrilled to be here," William replied. "And I look forward to meeting my new colleagues soon."

"Well, on that note," Father said, "why don't we take a brief tour of the campus, then, while we are so close by?"

"That would be delightful!" Lottie answered. "I have not seen the college since I was a girl."

Father motioned to the servants to transport their baggage in the second carriage. As expected, they had several trunks and bags. The rest of their belongings—their furniture and books and things—would arrive in a few weeks.

They boarded the open-air carriage and traveled the short distance up Cascade Avenue to the Colorado College campus. The group came to a wide, grassy lawn with a few academic buildings, one of which stood out for its magnificent architecture—Cutler Hall. It had been the first building on campus, and it was quite impressive. Completely made of stone, with arched windows and gables, it looked like it had been there for a hundred years, not just 26.

Father peeked over at William, whose mouth had dropped open in surprise. "Your letters, Palmer," he said, "do not do this place justice. I think I will be quite happy here indeed."

The party continued on to Glen Eyrie, and the girls were eager to show off the new-and-improved castle to their aunt. When she lived there in the old days, her brothers slept in hammocks in the tower room, they spent lazy summer days swimming in the Devil's Punch Bowl, and she had a Newfoundland named Prince.

Needless to say, Aunt Lottie was astounded by the changes.

"I—I cannot believe it, Uncle, I truly cannot," she said and hugged him again. "You have realized my dear sister's dream, every bit of it." She looked around at the Palmer girls with tears in her eyes. "I am at a loss for words."

"We are so thrilled you approve of it, Aunt Lottie!" Elsie exclaimed.

"I love to hear you call me 'Uncle,' dear Lottie," Palmer said. "It reminds me of times gone by."

Mrs. Simmons and Palmer showed the Sclaters to their quarters, a lovely room on the third floor with its own sitting room.

"We will be very comfortable here," Mr. Sclater said as he surveyed the room. "We do intend to keep our own home in a few short months' time, though, Uncle. We have been corresponding with an architect, and Elsie has been so kind to oversee it for us here."

"I understand," Palmer replied, "but you and Lottie are welcome here for as long as you need."

AUNT LOTTIE SPENT COUNTLESS hours that summer with the Palmer girls, having tea, paying visits to old friends, and going on short excursions into the mountains. She filled a void they so desperately needed filled. For Dorothy and Marjory, she had a welcome familiarity that felt so much like Mama. For Elsie, she was a best friend and confidant. Over time, Elsie's mood changed completely. She became her vibrant, happy self once more.

On a Tuesday in August, Aunt Lottie's architect, Thomas MacLaren, came to Glen Eyrie to meet with her and Elsie. While they poured over plans for the new house, Berty knocked softly on the drawing room door and delivered a letter to Elsie. It was from Leo.

She tore it open but could barely make out the words on the paper. It had apparently gotten lost in the mail for weeks, finally arriving after a mail sorter found it stuffed under a heat grate at the mail sorting facility. It had been dropped at some point and kicked under there. Soaked through, she could make out the postmark—July 1905, sent from Chicago—and Leo's name, but only a word or two here and there were still legible.

Elsie tucked the letter away and tried her best to pay attention to Mr. MacLaren's plans. After the architecture meeting, Elsie went straight to her room and sat down at her desk to write a letter to their mutual friends to inquire after Leo's Chicago address.

A week later, she was met with disappointment. Her friends informed her that Leo was now a wealthy man and traveled extensively all over the world. He had realized his dream of becoming a writer and spent months in Paris, a month or two in New York, a few weeks in India. He was notoriously difficult to nail down.

She set the letter from Leo aside and ignored it for now. She had closed the door on him, never to be reopened. But when she saw his name in ink on that ruined letter, something stirred deep within her heart. Why was he writing to her now, after all these years?

A few days later, a letter arrived to Glen Eyrie addressed to Elsie. She recognized the hand immediately and tore open the letter. Their mutual friends had written to him, it said, and, miraculously, their letter had been forwarded on to him. He had been living in Montana the past several months, in a cabin, writing.

As soon as he had received their letter, Leo wrote, he had sat down and composed the letter now in her hands. He instructed her not to reply to him, for he had booked a train ticket to Colorado Springs and would be arriving by the end of the week.

Elsie looked up from the letter into the face of Lanora, who was concerned by the frantic look on Elsie's face.

"Everything alright, Miss Elsie?" she asked.

"Ah, hello, Lanora, I did not see you there. Yes, I am fine. Just surprised, that is all."

"Very good," she replied as she curtsied and left the room.

Elsie hurried to her quarters and lightly shut the door behind her. She paced the room, balling her fists and muttering under her breath. "Why is he doing this? Doesn't he know I have closed that door? I have not heard from him in years. He was never serious about me before. What has changed?"

She took a minute to compose herself and left her quarters in search of Marjory. She found her in the music room at the piano. Elsie sat down next to her on the bench and laid her head gently on Marjory's shoulder. Marjory stopped playing and swiveled around on the bench, draping her long arms across her sister's lap.

"What is wrong, dear sister?" she said softly. "What has upset you?"

"Oh, Marjory," she sighed. "I do not know what to do. I have had a letter from Leo—"

"Surely not!" Marjory said loudly. "After all this time?"

"Yes … I know … and he is headed here."

"Here? To Glen Eyrie? Whatever for?"

"That is exactly what I am wondering, too, Marj."

THE END OF THE week arrived. Elsie had told Father and Dorothy about Leo's unexpected visit, and everyone was tense, wondering why he wanted to come for a visit and what exactly he planned to do. Dorothy and Marjory whispered as they discussed potential motives:

"Perhaps he borrowed something from Elsie years ago and wants to return it?" "Perhaps he really wants to speak with Father and not Elsie, for some business opportunity, maybe?"

The third motive they spoke out loud: "Perhaps he is in love with you, Elsie?" They could tell by the look on her face that she had pondered the same thing, too. Father, on the other hand, looked surprised by their suggestion.

"Well if he is, he will not receive permission from me."

"But Father," Marjory said, "perhaps he was immature and poor back then and did not feel worthy of our Elsie. Obviously, he has made his fortune now, and perhaps he has been thinking about Elsie all this time?"

"Have you thought about him, Elsie?" Father asked. "You seemed to have moved on years ago, but have you been harboring romantic feelings for him?"

Elsie thought about his letter announcing his engagement. She had never told anyone about it. "I admit I have not," Elsie said truthfully. "At least I thought I had not. Until I read his letter, and the memories came flooding back. He was my dear friend back in England."

"Well," Father replied. "He is due any minute, and we will just have to find out what he wants when he arrives."

MARJORY STOOD BY A window in the Book Hall that faced the Carriage House for what seemed like hours, while Elsie paced the floor. She stared at her portrait and thought back to her time with Leo in England. Her first impression of him had not been excellent, for he was loud and opinionated, and it bristled against her own strong personality. He was popular among women, even back then, but she was always his favorite companion.

They were thrown together often by their mothers, even serving as one another's dance partners on the off-chance that their cards were not filled. Over time, they became very close.

Now he was on his way to see her. How would her heart respond?

"Here he comes!" Marjory nearly shouted and grasped Elsie's hand. The Palmers lined up in the front hall to greet him. After a few moments, they heard a deep, masculine voice in the entryway, and they could hear Berty greet him and offer to remove his jacket and hat.

"Very kind, sir, thank you," came the deep voice again. Elsie drew in her breath and waited for the moment when she would see Leo for the first time in nearly 11 years.

A tall, handsome man stepped through the doorway and into the front hall. At once, Father stepped forward to shake his hand and welcome him to their home. Leo thanked Father profusely and made his way around the circle, shaking hands with each Palmer girl. When he made his way to Elsie, he stood for a moment in awe. She had changed so much, but she was as beautiful as ever.

Elsie was struck, too, by his altered appearance. He had always been handsome, but the years had been kind to him. He looked rugged— perhaps due to his recent time in Montana—but also refined, like the gentleman he was. Leo pulled her into an embrace.

"I have missed you so very much," he said into her curly, brown hair. Elsie appeared slightly embarrassed to be embracing him so informally, but she consoled herself with the fact that they were very old friends. And Father did not seem scandalized, which set her at ease even more.

Dorothy and Marjory crowded around him then, giving Elsie a moment to catch her breath. Her heart was beating a million miles a minute, and she felt slightly like she might pass out. What was wrong with her? Father looked her squarely in the eyes.

"Are you alright, darling?" he said and embraced her.

"Yes, Father, I am fine. Just feel a bit nervous for some reason."

"That is natural, my darling, to feel nervous seeing someone you have not seen in many years. Just do not allow it to cloud your thinking, my dear. We do not yet know his purpose in coming here."

"You are right, Father, thank you." Elsie let out her breath and closed her eyes for a moment. When she reopened them, she said, "I am better now."

Father and Elsie rejoined the group and led Leo to the parlor, where Mrs. Simmons had ordered the servants to lay a fine lunch of cold cut meats, cheeses, and bread.

After they had their fill of the spread, Father changed the subject. "We are so pleased to have you stay with us, Leo; it has been far too long since we saw you last. May I ask, do you have any special purpose in visiting us now?"

Leo smiled then and looked at Elsie for a brief moment. "I admit I had hoped to see you all in your new home in Colorado."

"Yes, but we have lived here for many years," Dorothy cut in. "Why now and not before?"

"Dos, do not be rude," Elsie said, embarrassed by her sister's brazen question.

"I apologize, Els, I am merely trying to ascertain Leo's purpose here—"

"As you should, Dorothy. I, myself, am slightly surprised to be welcomed so kindly to your home. I thought perhaps I had ruined our friendship forever with my thoughtlessness."

Elsie looked down at the floor then and seemed unsure of what to say. Marjory broke the silence. "Would you like to see your room?" She rang the bell for Mrs. Simmons, who motioned for Leo to follow her to a third-story guest room that overlooked Major Domo.

Elsie had chosen that room specifically for Leo, as it had one of the best views. It was close to the narrow servants' staircase, which led down near her own room on the floor below. She did not hope for anything unbecoming to happen, of course; she merely wanted to be able to converse with Leo in private during his stay. They had much to talk about.

THE NEXT MORNING, ELSIE thought it wise to allow Leo to rest from his long journey and ordered breakfast to be taken to his quarters.

Upon waking, he bathed and dressed and descended the grand staircase to find Elsie alone in the library. She appeared to be engrossed in a book, but as he watched her for a few moments, he noticed her eyes did not move across the page. He knew she was deep in thought.

He silently walked across the room and sat down next to her on the window seat. She smiled when she saw him. He reached for her hand and covered it with his own. Elsie's heart began to beat rapidly again. As he drew nearer, she could smell his musky cologne and noticed he had shaved his face. Close up, he looked just as she remembered him years ago—baby-faced and gentle.

"Leo, I—"

"Shhhh," he whispered. "Please allow me to speak first."

Elsie acquiesced with a glance.

"My dearest Elsie, I know I have been a cad. All those years ago, I promised to write you, to visit you, and instead I toyed with your heart. The day you left England was the worst day of my life, and I was angry with you for leaving. For the next several months, my pride prevented me from writing to you. I could not bear the thought that I was pining away while you were off making a new life for yourself, meeting lots of young men.

"I expected your engagement announcement every day for months, but when it never came I allowed myself a small modicum of hope. So I started to write to you, but I could never bring myself to post the letters. I knew in my heart I did not deserve you.

"And then I wrote you *the* letter. I am ashamed of it now. I told you I was engaged, but it was not true.

Elsie stared at him, wide-eyed and in horror. *How could he?*

"That was the only way I could move on. And I wanted to give you permission to move on, too."

"But Leo—"

"Let me finish, please, Elsie, let me finish." He cleared his throat and began again. "By then I had made my millions and traveled all over the world. I used my pain and funneled it into perfecting my craft. I wrote and wrote and wrote, thousands of pages. It was as if my heart had died, but my pen was burning with passion. Selfishly, I coveted the inspiration and made you into a villain in my mind. I believed that was the only way I could write with such fervor. You had to be my long-lost love."

Elsie felt confused, betrayed, worried.

"But then one day I woke up and the fervor was gone. I struggled to put pen to paper. I could barely journal. All of my friends told me I had a medical condition. So I wrote to you, hoping you would write back a scathing reply. But then I never heard from you.

"And when I received the letter from our friends in England, describing how my letter had only recently made its way to you, I could hardly believe it. I knew I had to come here and tell you how much I love you."

Leo paused then and looked at Elsie, to gauge her reaction. Elsie looked crestfallen, as if she had been slapped in the face.

"Why are you here?"

"I told you. Because I love you."

Elsie said nothing for several minutes. "It seems to me—" She cleared her throat. "It seems to me you are here merely because you need inspiration for your writing. Please tell me that is not true."

"That is not true at all, dearest Elsie. Not at all. I came here because I am in love with you. Yes, my writing is better when I am passionate about something, and I am passionate about you. Please tell me you love me, too, Els."

Elsie pondered this. She was not convinced his intentions were as pure as he claimed. But he did say he loved her. *Was that enough? Could she believe him? Why had he lied?*

"I need some air," she said and left the room, in search of Father. She knocked lightly on the door to his den.

"Father," she said as she opened the door. "Father, please help me. Leo has declared his love for me. He claims he has always loved me, ever since England."

"So that is why he came." Father thought for a long moment, laying his head back on his chair for a while as he considered the situation. Elsie watched him patiently. "Do you love him?" he finally said.

"Well, he also described how I fueled his passion for writing. I fear he only wants me now because he is in need of a muse."

"Did he say as much?"

"He insists that his motives are pure. He loves me. But I wonder."

"Darling, I can understand Leo's passionate nature. I, too, am a passionate man. When I met your mother, I felt sick with love. And her reciprocated love fueled my work, inspired me to take risks, and led me to build this castle. Without that passion, I would not have been able to create my empire. Perhaps Leo is the same way. Perhaps he needs a great passion to motivate him towards success. He is a writer, and writers are temperamental and reliant on fleeting inspiration to perform their craft well."

"It is not as simple as all that, Father. I do believe he loves me, but he lied to me."

Father rose slightly in his chair.

"No—" Elsie said and lifted her hand to stop him. "Please do not go to him."

"If he has lied to you, he must be made to leave."

"Father, I know I should have told you back then, but several years ago, Leo wrote to tell me he was engaged. I was so heartbroken and ashamed, I told no one."

"That scoundrel. How dare he."

"It was wrong, what he did. But for some reason, I am not upset."

"He does not deserve you, Els," Father stated, matter-of-factly.

"Perhaps not, but the truth is, I love him, too."

"But is it enough to build a marriage upon?"

Elsie did not reply. She stared into the fire, and after a few moments Father picked up his book again.

"I do not know," she finally said.

"Weigh your options, spend time in prayer, talk with your sisters, and then decide. We will stand by you no matter what you choose."

"Thank you, Father," Elsie said, kissed him on the forehead, and closed the door behind her.

She did not return to the library and to Leo, but instead walked out the front door. It was a fine day, cooler than it had been in weeks. She gathered her skirt and launched herself up onto the path behind the house and high-stepped through the tall prairie grass as she walked east.

Elsie rounded the bend in the path, and Pike's Peak came into full view, with the Garden of the Gods below. The contrast of blue sky, purple mountain, and bright red rock was stunning, a feast for the senses. She took a deep, lung-filling breath and exhaled through her nose, closing her eyes as she did so. Elsie reached up to unpin her hair, and it fell down in long tendrils past her shoulders. She raised her arms above her head, stretched out past the mother mountain and straight to God above.

THAT AFTERNOON, ELSIE WENT to the train station with Jesse to collect Aunt Lottie and Uncle William. They had been on a trip to New York, and, while they were away, the finishing touches were being completed on their new house.

In 1900, the pumpkin-growing Chambers family had to sell their beautiful farm, and Palmer knew he must buy it. At the time, he had no idea what he would use the land for, but after the Sclaters' arrival, it became clear. The property had several outbuildings and a house, but Palmer wanted Lottie to be able to build a new house of her own, to suit her own tastes.

It had taken months for Elsie to find a local architect who could create a home in the Cape Dutch style of South Africa. Lottie wanted white stucco, brown shutters, and interesting rooflines for the outside and Arts-and-Crafts-style dark wooden walls, low doorways, and a bright kitchen for the inside, with servants' quarters tucked up in the attic.

"I thought of a name for the house!" Lottie said to Elsie as they rode in the carriage. The Sclaters would move to the Chambers Ranch in a couple of weeks, but for now they planned to stay at Glen Eyrie.

"*Oooooh*. Tell me, tell me!"

"Think *Little Women*."

"You are naming it … Laurie?" Elsie guessed, half-joking. Lottie shook her head. "Baer House? Jo's Corner?"

"No and no. Keep guessing."

Quickly running out of ideas, Elsie sighed. Then it dawned on her. "Oh my! How perfect!"

"Orchard House!" the pair of them said in unison.

Lottie squealed and William rolled his eyes.

On the way to the castle, she filled Aunt Lottie in on the situation with Leo. She coveted her aunt's perspective. Father would be happy with whatever she decided because that was Father's way, so she needed Aunt Lottie to speak sense into the situation, to provide wise counsel.

William was Aunt Lottie's second husband. Her first marriage had been a total disaster that had ended in divorce. The only good thing to come from the match had been her two sons, Cyril and Eric, both of whom had grown into successful men. Aunt Lottie would have much wisdom about being married, as she had done it twice. While Uncle William dozed off, the pair discussed Elsie's options.

"Well, what kind of a man is he, this Leo?" Aunt Lottie said. "Is he decent?"

"He is, very. Our families dined together often back in England. Mama was extremely fond of him."

Aunt Lottie considered this for a moment and then replied, "If your mama liked him, I dare say we will, too. What you described before about his search for a muse, that is indeed interesting. I am inclined to agree with your father, although I believe your mama was much more to him than a mere muse."

"Indeed, Aunt," Elsie said.

Uncle William let out a loud snore then and started mumbling about birds.

Elsie laughed out loud and looked at her aunt. "He does this all the time," she remarked and laughed, too.

"In all seriousness, I cannot make the decision for you, Elsie. I try to consider what your mama would say. If she did, indeed, like him so very much when he was a boy, how different can he possibly be now?"

"I have made up my mind," Elsie said and exhaled slowly. "I will talk to him tonight."

"DO NOT TOY WITH me, Els," Leo said with a look of desperation on his face.

"I am not!" Elsie replied. "I am being completely serious."

Leo stared into the fireplace for a moment to watch the tendrils of smoke dance and curl. He had been enjoying a cigar by the fire before Elsie burst into the room, looking flushed and flustered. He broke into a huge smile. "The answer is yes?"

"The answer is yes. Yes, I will marry you."

"Marry you? But I did not—"

"Perhaps not, but that is your intention, is it not?"

"Well, yes, eventually, but—"

"Then it is settled," she said and clasped her hands together in her lap.

THAT NIGHT, AS ELSIE lay in bed, unable to sleep, her mind returned to their conversation by the fire. As she replayed the conversation, she started to feel nauseous. *Why does it feel like I have made a contractual agreement with him? Don't I love him? If I do, then why do I feel so ... uncertain?*

She could not help but feel somewhat overwhelmed by the events of the past couple of days. Leo had arrived, looking handsomer than ever, he had professed his undying love for her, and she accepted his hand, and ... *Marjory!*

She half-ran to the door and yanked it open, wrapping her robe around her as she tiptoed to her sister's room. *She will know how to help me.*

She rapped softly on Marjory's door until she heard a quiet "Come in." When Marjory saw the look of desperation on her sister's face, she motioned her over to the bed to sit down. Marjory had seen that look only one other time—the night Dorothy revealed Florenz's offer of marriage.

"Elsie? What is it?"

"I accepted Leo's hand."

Marjory's eyes widened in disbelief as she exclaimed, "He proposed! Why did you not tell me?"

"He did not propose, not exactly ..."

Marjory looked utterly confused by this. "Wait a moment. He did not propose?"

"He did not, but I made my intentions known, and he reciprocated, and we agreed to be married."

Marjory pondered this for a moment. At a loss for words, she blurted out the first thing that came to mind. "Wellesley and I are engaged."

Seeing her sister's look of incredulity, she hurried on. "I am sorry, Els, I was going to tell you tomorrow. He wrote to me just today to ask for my hand, and I accepted."

"That is wonderful news!" Elsie said and threw her arms around her sister. She pulled back and looked at Marjory, "You told him, then, about your condition?"

"I told him. He was ... gracious."

Elsie could sense that her sister did not want to discuss the matter further, so she simply said, "I am happy for you, Marj."

"Thank you, Els."

Marjory stared at her sister and noticed the sad look on her face. She knew what she must do. First thing tomorrow, she would find Leo.

MARJORY'S CHANCE DID NOT come until the following evening, for the daytime was quite taken up with the announcement of their engagement to the family, along with a visit to Orchard House with Aunt Lottie and Uncle William.

Father's reaction to the news surprised Elsie. She thought perhaps he would be upset that Leo had not asked him for his daughter's hand before the pair of them had discussed it, but Leo had been quite surprised by it, too, after all.

"I wish you both all the happiness in the world," he said and clapped Leo rather hard on the back. "I look forward to discussing your plans for the future at length at your earliest convenience."

"Father, Leo has plans to return to Chicago very soon," Elsie said.

Father looked at Leo, questioningly.

"Yes, sir, I have some business I must attend to. But I have every intention of corresponding regularly with Elsie. Perhaps we could correspond regularly, as well."

"I would like that, thank you," Father said.

As the conversation wore on, Elsie made her excuses and ascended the stairs to her bedroom. Leo stood up a few moments later, followed by Marjory.

On the first-floor landing, Marjory pulled him aside. "Leo," she said, "this is a bit awkward for me, and I do not quite know how to say it, but there is something you must know. Elsie has been through a lot. And she really wants to be married. She has often talked about the perfect marriage proposal, and your proposal, if you can call it that, was not the best. Do you understand?"

Leo, dumbstruck, nodded his head in agreement. Satisfied, Marjory turned and left.

From inside her room, Elsie heard footsteps on the stairs. She leaped from bed and tiptoed to the door to peek out. It was Leo. He smiled at her and walked over.

"I had hoped you would still be awake, Els. I wanted to say goodnight."

Elsie blushed and fiddled with a curl that had come loose. Leo stepped closer to her then and reached his hand up to her face, brushing the curl back.

"I love you, my darling," he said softly. "And I would like nothing more than for you to be my wife. I was a buffoon yesterday. I should have wrapped you in my arms, kissed you, and never let go."

He bent down and pressed his lips firmly on hers. She relaxed and leaned in to his kiss. Before she knew it, he pulled away from her and brushed her face lightly again.

When she looked into his eyes in that moment, she could see his heart. She no longer doubted his love for her. Perhaps his timing had been odd, and his delivery blunt, but without a doubt in her mind, he loved her. And she loved him.

Lying in bed, Elsie could still feel the weight of his lips on hers. It had been the perfect kiss. He left for Chicago two days later and remained there for several months, but he wrote to her every day, as promised. They discussed wedding plans and family news and began to dream about a shared future.

For once in her life, she felt free to dream. She had someone to catch her if she fell, and that gave her immense freedom. Elsie felt more confident than she ever had before, and it infused itself into every area of her life. While he was away, she took up old hobbies, visited animatedly with her friends and sisters, and poured herself into preparations for Marjory's wedding, and for her own. She was a new woman.

Chapter Eight

Some old-fashioned things like fresh air and sunshine are hard to beat.
LAURA INGALLS WILDER

FALL 1906
GLEN EYRIE

THE NEXT YEAR, FALL arrived and brought with it crisp evenings and aspen trees of beautiful yellow and orange. Father loved to explore the area on horseback during this time of year, when Pike's Peak had a dusting of snow, and the ground beneath became crunchy and firm.

On an afternoon in late October, Elsie made the short ride to Orchard House to have tea with Aunt Lottie. While she was away, Father asked Dorothy and Marjory to accompany him on a short horse ride to the Garden of the Gods and back. Their friend, Miss Miller, was visiting, so they invited her along, as well. He wanted to enjoy one of the last few fair weather days before a long winter. The girls happily

obliged and walked with Father to the Carriage House, where he
mounted Schoolboy, a beautiful bronco.

"Father, are you certain you want to take Schoolboy? He nearly
bucked you last week, remember?" Marjory said with concern in her
eyes.

"I know, darling, but I do love his spirit," he said and patted the
horse's hindquarters. "All will be well."

As they trotted out of the Glen Eyrie property and headed the few
miles south, they discussed plans for the upcoming Christmas party for
the townschildren, and Dorothy talked about her improvements for
this year's festivities.

The four of them crested a large hill and began to descend into the
valley below when Marjory let out an ear-piercing scream. Dorothy and
Miss Miller whipped around to see Father lying on his back on the
ground near Schoolboy. The horse had stumbled on the way down the
steep decline and thrown Father over his head.

They dismounted quickly and ran to his side, screaming his name as
they attempted to survey the damage. Father could not talk or move his
limbs, but his eyes darted back and forth between their faces with a
look of immense fear and pain. Dorothy began to run down the trail to
find help, and in a stroke of God's mercy found William Otis, a local
banker and heir to the Otis elevator fortune, who was taking a joyride
nearby in his new car.

Mr. Otis climbed out of his car and rushed to Father's side. With
the girls' help, they lifted Father and placed him in the backseat of the
car. Mr. Otis drove quickly but carefully back to Glen Eyrie, as the girls
followed behind on horseback.

When they approached the gatehouse, Dorothy rode ahead and
alerted Jesse Bass and Berty to what happened, and the pair of them
ran up to the main house. With the help of Mr. Otis and Florenz, they
carried Father up to his room. Mrs. Simmons frantically sent word to
Dr. Swan, Father's physician, and he arrived within the hour. Beloved
Dr. Jameson had retired a few years previously.

Without saying a word, Dorothy ran out the door, mounted her horse again, and galloped in the direction of Orchard House. At the gate, she disembarked and knocked loudly on the door. The servant looked panic-stricken as she swung open the door.

"What is it, Miss?" the servant said.

"Please take me to my sister and aunt," she said and ran inside. "Quickly!"

Elsie and Aunt Lottie heard the commotion from the parlor and stepped into the entryway to find Dorothy in dire straits. When her eyes met Elsie's, she burst into tears.

"It's Father, Els! Come now!"

Elsie did not need any more urging. Aunt Lottie yelled to the servant to fetch the carriage, and the three quickly raced to the Glen.

When they arrived, Elsie tried to enter Father's quarters, but she was stopped at the door by Dr. Swan.

"Your father is too fragile to see anyone right now, Miss Elsie. Allow me to examine him, and then I will permit you entry."

Aunt Lottie and the Palmer girls paced the floor while Dr. Swan performed his extensive examination. They clung to each other and sobbed, worried sick that Father might not survive.

After a couple of hours, Dr. Swan delivered the prognosis: Father's neck had been broken, and he suffered complete paralysis of both motor and sensory functions below the neck. He warned the girls to prepare for the worst—Father might not make it through the night.

They were devastated. With the doctor's permission, they visited Father in his room. Dr. Swan had given him a strong sedative and placed a padded collar around his neck. They were shocked by his altered appearance. No longer the gentle giant, he now looked like a small, fragile, broken man.

FATHER SURVIVED THE first night, but he looked no better by the light of morning. Still strongly sedated, the girls took turns sitting by his bedside—praying, reading to him, stroking his hand. They were separated from him only to allow Dr. Swan his hourly examination and administration of medicines.

Dr. Swan had ordered him to lie flat on his back at all times, so they hired live-in nurses to help bathe him and change his catheter. As the days passed, Father slowly began to regain some of his strength.

Over the next few weeks, Aunt Lottie and Uncle William were instrumental in organizing Palmer's care and providing support to the girls. Their son Cyril traveled from New York to stay at the castle for a short while, as did Eric, who was stationed in Egypt with the British Army. Aunt Maud moved in to Glen Eyrie with her three small daughters. Suddenly the house felt full of life, even if a bit more cramped than usual.

As Father began to regain his strength, he began to despise being confined to his room, flat on his back, so Lottie and the Palmer girls took turns reading his correspondence aloud—letters of business and some of encouragement—and writing out his replies. All of Queen's siblings wrote to him regularly and sent him silly cards. Aunt Maud's small daughters loved Father, even though he could not play with them. He told them stories and jokes, and they could often be heard squealing with delight.

Cyril and Eric had not been back to Colorado in almost 15 years, so they were astonished at the vast improvements the Palmers had made to the castle. They took up residence in the Tower Room, just as their uncles had in the old days, and spent hours exploring the vast home.

WINTER 1907
GLEN EYRIE

AS DR. SWAN OVERSAW Father's improvements, he decided it best to pass the baton of his extensive care on to a younger and more able-bodied Dr. Henry Watt. A native-born Englishman, Dr. Watt had attended medical school while abroad and immigrated to Colorado only a couple of years before, seeking better working conditions and higher pay. He found himself in wild and unbridled Colorado, which, oddly enough, suited him to a tee.

He had found employment in Colorado Springs as a resident physician, and he was due to arrive at Glen Eyrie by the end of the week. After some not-so-subtle probing, Dr. Swan confirmed the girls' suspicions that he was relatively young, around 35 years of age, and a bachelor.

"*Oooooh*," Marjory said and nudged Dorothy in the ribs. Dorothy rolled her eyes.

"Just because you did not want to marry Florenz does not mean you will never marry," Marjory said and sighed.

"I do not mean to marry, Marjory. Accept it and move on."

"Fine," she said, in mock anger.

The Palmer girls sat around the breakfast table early that morning. Leo was due within the hour. It had been nearly four months since he was last in Colorado Springs, and he had yet to see Father in his current state.

Elsie was dressed in her prettiest frock—a light blue, striped dress with white lace trimming. Lanora had curled her hair before pinning it into an elaborate updo. For the first time in weeks, she felt well.

After breakfast, Elsie climbed the stairs and knocked softly on Father's bedroom door. He told her to enter, and she swung open the door. A nurse bustled about, preparing Father for the day. Elsie watched for a moment as the nurse gently bent Father forward at the waist to change his shirt. Her movements looked effortless.

Father's deep voice snapped her back to the present, and she smiled as he very slowly and carefully turned his head to see her. He had improved so much in just a few short months, and, with Dr. Watt's care, hopefully he would begin to make daily improvements.

"My darling," he said in that old familiar way. "How beautiful you look. Come closer so I can see you better."

She did as she was told, and he smiled broadly at her. "Today is the day."

"Today's the day. He is very eager to see you, Father."

"And I him. His presence will bring me comfort," he said and looked pensive for a moment. Elsie tried hard to not look completely surprised by this. He cleared his throat and continued, "I so miss visiting with people. I used to go to the club or the Antlers for lunch nearly every day. And all afternoon long, business contacts and friends would be in and out of this house. Now none of them dare come here. I might as well be dead."

"Oh, Father." Elsie stroked his arm. "That is very untrue. Your friends have stayed away to give you time to heal. Nothing more. In no time, the house will be full of them again, you will see."

"I suppose," Father said, unconvincingly.

They chatted for a few moments more about the day's forthcoming activities and arrangements. Elsie had mapped out the whole day. First, they would greet Dr. Watt, who would then perform an examination of Father in order to choose the best method of continuing care and recovery. After that, the doctor, Leo, and the girls would take dinner together.

Elsie was jolted by a knock at Father's door. Mrs. Simmons had come to announce the arrival of her long-anticipated guest. As she descended the stairs, she saw Leo strip off his overcoat and hat and place them in Berty's arms. *My, how handsome he looks,* she thought and smiled to herself.

Leo greeted her with a kiss and said, "Hello, beautiful. I have missed you."

She took him to see Father then, who perked up at the sight of Leo.

"Leo," he said and slowly attempted to turn his neck towards the door.

"No, don't trouble yourself on my account," Leo said and gently patted Palmer's shoulder. "Thank you for your correspondence these past several months. Your detailed accounts made me feel like I never left, that I was right here with you … at home."

Elsie felt touched by his words. *Home.*

"You recognized Elsie's hand, no doubt," Father said. "She has been corresponding on my behalf."

"I assumed as much, yes," Leo replied.

Father and Leo chatted for a long while, and Leo related his business ventures in Chicago and New York. Father listened with rapt attention.

"Well, you returned home on a most opportune day. A Doctor Watt is expected any moment. He will be facilitating my care, and he has developed some innovative therapy he is eager to try out on me." Father motioned to Leo to come in closer, as he said, "I must admit I do not share his eagerness, but so be it!"

Leo chuckled and looked over at Elsie. Just then they heard a soft knock on the bedroom door. It was Lanora, announcing Dr. Watt's arrival.

She and Leo gathered the other girls, Aunt Maud, and the Sclaters, and they all descended the stairs to meet the miracle doctor.

As they rounded the corner of the staircase, before them stood a tall, handsome man with a bushy mustache and small spectacles. He had a kind face, and he smiled at them as he nervously clutched his medical bag. Elsie glanced over at Dorothy, who did not seem fazed at all. Marjory, though, had a big smile on her face.

Marjory spoke first and offered her hand to the doctor, who bowed slightly and said, "Very pleased to make your acquaintance. I am Doctor Henry Watt."

Dorothy offered to escort the doctor up to Father's room, chatting with him about the medical profession and all that it entails. Marjory and Elsie followed her lead, and when they approached Father's door, they gently knocked and the nurse let them in.

"AH, DOCTOR WATT, PLEASE do come in," Father said in his gentle but commanding tone.

Dr. Watt stepped forward confidently to his bedside. He seemed awestruck for a brief moment but then grasped Father's hand very firmly and said, "I am so very pleased to make your acquaintance, sir."

"Please, no formalities here. You can call me 'Palmer.'"

"I couldn't possibly—"

"I insist. You will be poking and prodding me, and I cannot conceive of you calling me 'sir' while doing so."

"Very well!" Dr. Watt said with a broad smile on his face. He looked over at the girls, who chuckled.

Father asked his daughters to leave the room while the doctor performed his examination. Dr. Watt requested a bowl of hot water from one of the servants and pulled a large bar of soap out of his medical bag. Father wondered what was wrong with the soap in his lavatory, but he did not ask.

He watched in amazement as Dr. Watt rolled up his sleeves to the elbow, then began to scrub them thoroughly with the bar of soap, dunking them into the bowl of water periodically. He scrubbed in between his fingers, under his fingernails, and around his elbows. Dr. Watt did not say a word as he performed his ritual, but after about 10 minutes he dried his hands on a fresh towel and went to Father's bed.

Father was right—he poked, prodded, drew blood, and asked him a myriad of questions about his recovery and care thus far. He recorded everything in a small, black leather journal. Father insisted that Dr. Swan had already tested his blood, but Dr. Watt claimed to have a special method of testing blood that he himself had perfected in his laboratory.

Father felt completely comfortable and easy with the new doctor, a fact which pleased him greatly. Dr. Swan was a talented physician, but he lacked a certain bedside manner that seemed to come naturally to this young doctor.

The examination took several hours, during which Uncle William and Leo enjoyed cigars in Father's den. Elsie, Dorothy, Aunt Maud, and Aunt Lottie sat by the fire and played cards in the music room. Marjory was seated at the piano, hard at work learning a new piece of music Father had given her before his fall—a movement from Richard Wagner's *Tristan und Isolde*.

When he was finished, Dr. Watt found the women in the music room and plopped down into a comfy chair, utterly exhausted.

"Pardon my informality," he said, "but I'm really quite tired." After a few moments, he realized someone was playing the piano and turned to look at Marjory. "That is really quite beautiful," he said and laid his head against the back of the chair and closed his eyes.

Several minutes later, Marjory finished the movement, closed the piano lid, and sat down next to Dr. Watt. He opened his eyes and said again, "Pardon my informality."

"We don't mind at all, do we?" Marjory said, looked around at her sisters, and then smiled at him.

"You are finished with your examination, then?" Elsie asked Dr. Watt.

He sat up straighter in his chair a little and said, "Yes. Your father is a very brave man. The procedures I performed on him today are not particularly comfortable, but he bore it with strength and composure. He really makes a wonderful patient."

"Father is a superior man. In all ways. He does not flinch in the face of pain or danger, but he is terribly kind and gentle when you get to know him," Dorothy remarked.

"I do not doubt it," Dr. Watt replied. "I have admired your father from afar, and I am honored to be working for him now."

They looked quite pleased at his remarks about their beloved Father. They were all eager for his recovery.

"Do you expect he will be able to learn to walk again?" Dorothy asked after a short pause. "He would so dearly love to walk."

Dr. Watt looked serious for a moment but then returned to smiling once more. "If it be God's will. From a medical standpoint, however, the prognosis is not good. He will most likely remain paralyzed."

Dorothy and the others looked crestfallen. Dr. Watt hurried on and said, "But that does not mean he cannot live a full and happy life."

Elsie let out a loud breath, and Dr. Watt turned to look at her. "I apologize, it is just that I am so relieved to hear you say that. We have been so worried about Father's spirits. Most days, he stares at his bedroom wall and refuses to receive anyone but the maids and the doctor. Other days, he rallies and permits us entry."

"Do not be alarmed by his behavior, Miss Elsie. It is quite normal for an injury of this type. Your Father was an active and social man. In time, he will return to those things. But his recovery cannot be rushed."

Dorothy looked around at her sisters and asked, "How long?"

"Six months, maybe sooner. Under my care, and with the help of so many modern inventions to assist him, he should be able to return to his favorite activities soon. He will most likely be unable to mount a horse, but there are others ways to travel and take in the sights these days."

"How?" Elsie inquired.

"Well, he could get an automobile."

"Oh no, that will not do. My father detests automobiles," she explained. "He believes they are wholly unsafe. He always preferred horses. Rather ironic in light of his injury."

Dr. Watt only shrugged, but the wheels in Elsie's brain started spinning. Could she convince Father to purchase an automobile?

After dinner, Mrs. Simmons escorted Dr. Watt to his quarters. She led him to an elegantly furnished suite with windows facing west towards the mountains. He noticed his room was directly across the hallway from the youngest Miss Palmer, and he smiled to himself.

LIFE AT GLEN EYRIE soon settled into a routine. Dr. Watt performed his inspections in the morning, checking for bed sores and changing Father's catheter. Then he took lunch with Father in his sitting room, and they chatted about world news, politics, literature, and many other topics. Often, Uncle William would join them, and the three would have an animated discussion about the future of Colorado Springs, new medical inventions, and so forth.

After lunch, Dr. Watt changed Father's catheter again and ordered him to nap for a few hours. During this time, Dr. Watt explored the castle and the grounds, or took a quick trip into town to look after some of his other patients. He arrived back to Glen Eyrie in the afternoons and performed his second inspection of the day. After doing so, he dressed for dinner, which he took with the Palmer girls, Leo, the Sclaters, and Aunt Maud in the dining room. The group often enjoyed reading, replying to correspondence, or playing cards in the evenings, but Dr. Watt often took this time to record the day's happenings in his medical journal.

On one particular evening, Dr. Watt sat hunched over a small desk, feverishly writing in his journal. Elsie discreetly watched him, but Dorothy rose from her seat near the fire and walked over to him.

"May I?" she asked and motioned to the wooden chair beside him.

"Yes, of course," he replied and watched as she took a seat. She did not say anything at first, so Dr. Watt awkwardly continued to write as she looked on.

Eventually she broke the silence and said, "What is it you record in your journal so faithfully?"

Dr. Watt was pleased by her interest in his affairs and pushed the journal towards her. He showed her what a typical entry looked like, and commented on what bits of information he chose to record each day.

"I typically record your father's energy levels, his physical appearance, and any improvements, as well as his mood," he explained. "I also note any changes in my routine inspection or any new sores or bruises. It's fascinating to see how much your father improves each day, but it's even more wonderful to read the changes over the course of a week or a month. Hence the journal. It's my lifeline."

"The study of medicine intrigues me very much, Doctor Watt," Dorothy said. "I have always gravitated to the sick and injured among us, and I find God has used me many times to comfort those in need."

"I can see you are compassionate, Miss Dorothy, and that is something most doctors lack," Dr. Watt replied. "If you have a drive to help people and an interest in learning about medicine, maybe you should study to become a nurse."

Elsie and Marjory both perked up at the doctor's words of advice for their sister. They both knew Dorothy longed to make a difference in the world, and becoming a nurse might be the perfect way to do so.

"Maybe I will."

AS THE WEEKS PASSED, Palmer grew stronger and stronger under Dr. Watt's expert care. When he was first injured, he had no control over his body from the neck down. But after only a couple months of intensive therapy, he began to regain small movements in his neck and shoulders. This thrilled Palmer and gave him incredible hope.

They had an elevator installed inside the house, to allow Father access to his favorite spots—the library and his den. This small improvement raised his spirits even more.

Dr. Watt's unusual method of care began to gain attention with physicians far and wide. Several prominent doctors from Denver and even a few as far away as St. Louis were eager to witness his routines and made provisions to stay at Glen Eyrie for a short time. They were fascinated by Dr. Watt's method of scrubbing his hands and also his unorthodox way of keeping a journal to track Palmer's progress. The physicians asked numerous questions and insisted on being present during all of Dr. Watt's daily checkups.

Palmer entertained the physicians in his typical way—with lots of laughter and fun. He grew quite used to their presence at the castle and felt disappointed to see them leave. Elsie observed her father's altered behavior after their departure and knew it pained him to be excluded from the comings and goings of not only Glen Eyrie but Colorado Springs itself. His friends had started to visit him again, but he needed more. He needed to get out.

"DOS!" ELSIE SHOOK HER sister awake later that night. "I have decided."

"Ugh, Els!" Dorothy moaned and rolled over. She reached for the covers but Elsie kept them out of her reach.

"Don't make me get the bucket."

Often, Elsie was struck with brilliant ideas in the middle of the night. She would lie awake for a while before bolting out of bed and rushing to Dorothy's side. She did not particularly care whether Dos had been asleep for hours; she needed her full attention—now.

Usually, Dorothy would play along and wake up to hear her sister's enthusiastic idea, but sometimes she needed a little more … persuading. That is when Elsie got the bucket near the fireplace, filled it part-way with cold water, then dipped her fingers into it and let the freezing water *drip-drip-drip* from her fingertips onto her sister's warm face. This method was quite effective. Dorothy would bolt upright and even occasionally let out a small scream, often accompanied with an "Elsie!"

"What is it? What could be so important? I was having such a pleasant dream," Dorothy said, pretending to be upset.

Elsie laughed and placed a small candle on the bedside. The castle had electricity in every room—even the servants' quarters—but at night the girls still preferred to use candles.

"I want to buy Father an automobile." Elsie paused and waited for her sister's reaction. "Did you hear me?"

Dorothy took her time responding, a small payback for Elsie's impertinence. "Father will hate it."

"Yes, yes, I know he always says that, but think. He is desperate to be out and about again, and an automobile will be his freedom."

"Hmm," Dorothy pondered. "You have a point. But how would he drive it?"

"I've worked that all out," Elsie replied. "Doctor Watt told me about an auto he saw once in an exhibition. It has front seats for a driver, but the back is fitted for a reclining wheelchair. So Father could recline in comfort but still admire the view, traverse his favorite spots, and visit his friends!" Elsie smiled and looked very pleased with herself.

Dorothy hugged her sister. "That's brilliant. Honestly, I wish I'd thought of it myself. How do you come up with things like that?"

"Just natural intelligence," she said and smiled.

"And an unwavering love for Father."

THE NEXT DAY, ELSIE enlisted the help of Marjory, Berty, and Dr. Watt in organizing the logistics of a contraption that would make Father happy. It had to be both luxurious enough to replace horse-riding in Father's heart and comfortable enough to allow him to make longer treks if he saw fit. Elsie contacted the Stanley Steamer company and explained Father's situation to them.

They sent her a blueprint of a custom-made automobile, which she consulted over with Dr. Watt, who required various improvements to be made to ensure Father's safety. He also discreetly measured Father and sent the specifications back to the automobile company. They sent a second round of blueprints a few weeks later, and this time it looked perfect. Marjory chose a red leather interior with white trim. It had to be steam-driven to operate well in the high altitude.

Surprisingly, after only nine weeks, Elsie received notice that the completed automobile had been shipped to the Denver and Rio Grande Depot. She sent Berty and Jesse Bass to retrieve it.

Back at the castle, she gathered her sisters, Aunt Lottie, and the staff and assembled them near the front door. When she saw Berty slowly drive up the sloping road, she ran into music room and urged Father to close his eyes.

"Wha—"

"Just close them. Trust me."

With Berty's help, Elsie wheeled Father out into the hallway, through the front door, and parked him next to the small drive.

"OK, open!" she yelled. Father slowly opened his eyes, which became as large as lemons at the sight before him. "It's an automobile, Father. For you."

Father looked around at her but could not seem to form any words.

He was shocked. He asked Dr. Watt to wheel him closer to the automobile. Father ran his hand along the door and around the handle. He peered inside the windows and admired the leather interior.

"This is a fine machine," he said.

"Father, I know it is not the same as riding your beloved horses," Elsie said, "but we hope this will bring you joy."

His eyes betrayed his skepticism, but he chose to be optimistic. "Thank you, my darling."

"Would you like to try it?" Dr. Watt stepped forward and laid his hand on Father's shoulder.

"I would, yes."

"Allow me." Dr. Watt, with the help of Berty and Uncle William, slowly lifted Father out of his wheelchair and into the reclining chair in the automobile. They strapped him in securely, and Dr. Watt climbed into the driver's seat.

"Where to, sir?" Dr. Watt asked in an exaggerated English accent. The girls giggled.

"Take me—" Father said and paused for a moment. "Take me to the Garden."

Elsie looked worried and bent down to whisper in Father's ear. "Is that wise, Father? We do not want to upset you."

"I insist," he said. "I need to go back."

DR. WATT SLOWLY DROVE the automobile up the sloping grade to the entrance to the Garden of the Gods, while the Palmer girls followed behind on horseback. They exchanged worried glances, preoccupied with the sadness Father undoubtedly felt. It had been months since his accident, and in that time he had not left the house. But the girls feared this impromptu excursion to the scene of the accident would send him into a downward spiral.

When they crested the hill overlooking the red-spired valley, the girls trotted up next to the auto and dismounted. Dr. Watt wheeled

Palmer out and adjusted his wheelchair into a sitting position. Elsie's throat closed slightly as she surveyed her father's face. *Will he be overcome with emotion?* she thought.

To her surprise, Father sighed and smiled. "What a beautiful sight," he said. "Isn't it, darlings?"

Dorothy laid her hand on his shoulder. Then Elsie bent down to kiss his cheek. Marjory lingered behind, until Father beckoned her forward.

"It is alright," Father said, bravely. Tears fell from Marjory's eyes, soft and silent. Elsie was touched by her usually composed sister's display of emotion. Marjory burst into a sob and ran forward to kiss Father. When she straightened up, Dr. Watt was staring directly at her. She held his gaze for a few seconds then ran to him, arms outstretched.

"Doctor Watt," she said into his collar. "Thank you."

When she pulled away, she held his gaze again, this time for a while longer. Dr. Watt looked utterly baffled. Marjory had been friendly to him, but he had no idea this composed, orderly woman had such depth of feeling. He was wonderstruck.

Elsie noted his look of shock and turned away, embarrassed to witness the tender moment between them.

Marjory rejoined her sisters, and the whole party was silent as they gazed at the magnificent view. The imposing, purple-blue mountain peak contrasted perfectly with the red of the rock formations to create a picturesque scene. Elsie wished she could remember this moment forever. Only a few months ago, she thought she would lose Father, but now she knew deep inside that he would be alright.

SUMMER 1907

"I HAVE THE MOST brilliant idea! Really, Elsie, you will be quite proud of me," Father exclaimed one summer afternoon as they sat together in the library.

His attitude was improving daily, but she was surprised to hear the animation in his voice. It reminded her of the way he used to be, before the accident.

"What is it, Father?" she inquired.

"I received a letter a few days ago from a member of my old cavalry regiment. It is the thirty-fifth anniversary, you know. Anyway, he said they intend to have a reunion and wrote to invite me. Of course I would not be able to attend, but that's when it hit me!"

Father paused for a moment until Elsie motioned with her head for him to continue.

"Why not have the reunion here!"

"That would be marvelous! We would be thrilled to meet your war friends, and no doubt we have the space to accommodate them—"

"Not exactly," Father cut across her.

"Well, they cannot just stay in town, they must stay here!" she insisted.

"All two-hundred and eighty of them, darling?" Father said and cracked a smile.

Elsie gasped and replied, "I had no idea there were so many! How can so many still be alive?"

"I was one of the youngest in the bunch, but many of them have survived to old age, I am happy to report. Come, let us discuss the plan. We only have a couple of months to get everything ready."

AFTER MUCH PREPARATION, INCLUDING the coordination of lodging for all of the veterans, catering for the week-long reunion, and copious travel arrangements, the first day of the reunion finally arrived.

Father had arranged for his regiment to visit Colorado College, Pike's Peak, and the Garden of the Gods, and spend the afternoons and evenings on the lawn or in the Book Hall at Glen Eyrie. Weeks ago, he had asked Berty to organize his war memorabilia and to polish his medals, including his Medal of Honor.

He also asked Mrs. Simmons to unpack his old uniform from the war trunk and press it. Father would be unable to don the uniform trousers, but he intended to wear the jacket, with all of his medals pinned perfectly to it.

The veterans arrived in Colorado Springs on a special 10-car train. The majority of them still resided in Pennsylvania, where the regiment was formed all those years ago. Others made the trip from as far away as California and Washington State.

Thousands of townspeople, in addition to the entire Palmer family and the Sclaters, lined the streets around the Depot to welcome them to Colorado Springs. The party of veterans walked to the nearby Antlers Hotel, where most of them planned to stay, and then on to Colorado College, where the remaining 50 or so would lodge for the week.

The next morning, Palmer met his old comrades to give them a tour of downtown, while the town prepared an elaborate parade in their honor. Half a dozen bands lined up to march down Pikes Peak Avenue, with Palmer in his white Stanley Steamer leading the way. The veterans lined up in groups of four and marched together under their old banner. Crowds gathered along the road to watch them pass, throwing bouquets of flowers. What a spectacle it was.

That evening, they all gathered in the Book Hall at Glen Eyrie, laughing, eating, drinking—for the first time ever, Father allowed alcohol—and reminiscing about the war.

Dr. Watt helped Father through it all, wheeling him about and adjusting his chair when needed. Father was a great host. He told several funny stories about near-misses with cannon fire and "those rascal Confederates." He was completely in his element; the life of the party once more. The girls observed the festivities from the choir loft, where they discussed Father's amazingly improved spirits.

"Who knew all it would take to bring Father back from the brink was a party with some old comrades?" Marjory said.

"Old, indeed!" Dorothy retorted and laughed.

"Look at him," Elsie said. "I have never seen him this happy before.

Not before the accident, not ever. Do you not agree? He is completely altered."

Marjory and Dorothy watched Father as he told his stories and poked fun at his comrades.

"I love seeing him like this," Marjory said.

After a few minutes, Dr. Watt joined them in their hiding place. He sat down next to Marjory and whispered something into her ear, and Elsie's eyes immediately shot Dorothy a knowing look. To Elsie's disappointment, Dorothy just looked confused. *How dense can you be, Dos?* she thought.

An hour later, Marjory stood up and walked to the spiral staircase. Dr. Watt hurried behind her, gently grabbed her elbow, and said, "Permit me to assist you." He walked slowly behind her, supporting her as she made her way down.

At the bottom, she turned and looked at him. "Thank you," she said. "Sometimes I become dizzy."

Dorothy and Elsie descended the stairs behind them, and they hung back a moment, allowing Marjory and Dr. Watt to continue down the long hallway. They could hear them discussing Marjory's illness, and Dr. Watt suggested a new herbal tea for her to try. Dorothy whispered to Elsie, "What was that look? Earlier, in the choir loft."

"I believe Watt is in love with her," she whispered.

"What? Surely not. He knows full well she is engaged."

"An engagement rarely does much to deter a man when he is in love."

Dorothy looked pensive as she replied, "Does she love him?"

"I am not sure. Sometimes I think I see it in her eyes, and other times not. She used to talk about Wellesley constantly, do you remember? Not so anymore."

Dorothy gasped then, which caused Marjory to turn around to see her sisters several paces behind them.

Elsie motioned to Marjory to turn back around. Dorothy whispered, "I do believe you are right. Oh my. Poor Wellesley."

THAT NIGHT, AS MARJORY sat up reading, she heard a soft rap on her door. Believing it to be one of her sisters, she did not bother to wrap a shawl around herself and opened the door to find Dr. Watt.

"Oh, my!" she said and quickly closed the door. She reached for her shawl and haphazardly wrapped it around her shoulders, pulling it closed across the front. She glanced at herself in the mirror, then turned and opened the door again to find that Dr. Watt had disappeared.

She tiptoed across the hall to his door and knocked gently. Dr. Watt opened it, looked her full in the face, and smiled. Struck by his steady gaze, which betrayed his depth of emotion, she said nothing.

Dr. Watt spoke first. "Marjory," he said and paused to clear his throat. "I merely wanted to … that is, I wondered if you might permit me … I do not quite know what to say," he said awkwardly.

Marjory reached up and lightly touched his hand, urging him to go on.

"I have lain awake these past few nights," he continued, "my mind full of thoughts … of you. That is, your condition."

Marjory was confused, disappointed. "Oh. Thank you, Doctor Watt. I do appreciate your kind attentions."

Dr. Watt looked for a moment as if he wanted to confess something but said instead, "I have some ideas about how to improve your energy. Perhaps we can begin tomorrow?"

"That would be … fine, thank you," Marjory said and walked back to her room. When she closed the door behind her, she sat down on her bed and stared into the distance for a moment, her mind racing. *What does Doctor Watt feel for me? Is it merely doctorly concern for an invalid? Then why the tender looks, the whispers in my ear?*

She reached across the bed and blew out her candle, plunging the room into darkness.

ON THE LAST DAY of the reunion, the veterans gathered on the lawn at

Glen Eyrie, along with the Palmer girls and Father's beloved Great Dane, Yorick, for a photograph. The party said their goodbyes, and shortly after, all 280 were aboard the train that would take them home.

After the regiment's departure, life at Glen Eyrie returned to normal. To Elsie's surprise, Father remained in high spirits long after they left. He began to take more frequent automobile rides into town and to his old stomping grounds. He hired a mechanic, coincidentally named Glen Eyrie Martin, who quickly became his chauffeur, in addition.

More and more, his old business colleagues and friends visited him at home and regaled him with news about the railroads and their expansion endeavors.

Elsie resumed wedding planning with renewed vigor. Once they decided on January 20th for the date, everything suddenly became full-steam ahead. Marjory was an enormous help in that department, though, and they soon booked all of the necessary appointments to begin choosing flowers, a cake, a dress, and countless other details.

Leo and Elsie decided to have the ceremony performed at Glen Eyrie, in the Book Hall. With its tall windows and abundant view of the surrounding trees and rock formations, it was a perfect spot. She imagined rows of white chairs, with a platform at the east end, where Leo would stand as she made her way down the aisle.

She asked Dorothy and Marjory, of course, to be her bridesmaids, and to Elsie's surprise, Dorothy agreed without much persuading.

DECEMBER 1907
GLEN EYRIE

AS CHRISTMAS APPROACHED, THEY took a break from wedding planning to focus on the annual celebration with the townschildren.

This year, they had more children than ever before, but they still managed to pick out and purchase a small gift for each one.

When the children arrived that evening, Elsie had a curious feeling that it would be their last Christmas celebration of the kind at Glen Eyrie. Father's health improved every day, but she knew things were about to change once she got married. Dorothy mentioned several times a program in London that specialized in training high-bred girls as nurses. Father looked sad each time the subject was broached, but Elsie knew Dorothy longed for England. And she would make a wonderful nurse.

All of the servants attended the festivities—Berty, Mrs. Simmons, Anna and Lanora, even Florenz. It was like a big reunion of sorts, everyone merry and well-fed. Elsie made a point to capture the moment in her mind's eye, to pull out once in a while to remember those good days.

AFTER CHRISTMAS, THE BIG day was right around the corner, and Elsie started to prepare herself for what would be an enormous change. She would be leaving her sisters, her home, and her beloved Father. All would be different, and she did not know yet whether different would equal good. She trusted in her love for Leo, but she felt a sense of grief in the face of such a transition.

Elsie had spent the past 35 years as a single woman, and even though her courtship with Leo had taught her how to take another's needs and wishes into consideration, she could not help but feel that she was losing her freedom.

Leo arrived at Glen Eyrie two weeks before the wedding, just in time to visit the local tailor shop to have a new coat and tails made for him. He and Elsie discussed last-minute honeymoon plans at length each day. They decided a week in New York, a month or two in Italy, and ending the trip in England sounded absolutely perfect, and Leo arranged the travel and accommodations.

Everything was ready.

Chapter Nine

There is no charm equal to the tenderness of the heart.
JANE AUSTEN

JANUARY 20, 1908
GLEN EYRIE

THE DAY DAWNED JUST as a wedding day ought to—clear, cool, and crisp. The guests had all arrived, the floral arrangements were in place, and the groom had the rings safely tucked in his breast pocket.

Phooo. Elsie breathed nervously as Lanora styled her hair. "Should I be *this* nervous?" she said to no one in particular.

Her sisters sat on the bed nearby, waiting their turn to be coiffed and primped by Lanora's measured hand. Anna had already applied their makeup, and their dresses were ready and waiting for the right moment.

"If it were my wedding day, I would be dead on the floor," Dorothy replied and Marjory threw her a glance.

"Do not listen to her, Els," Marjory said. "Today will be perfect. We have planned it down to the last detail. Everything will go smoothly."

"Thank you, sweet sister," Elsie said and smiled at her. "Have either of you seen Leo this morning? He is awake, is he not?"

Marjory stood up from the bed then and crossed the room to the dressing table. "He is awake, everyone is awake and dressed. The guests are here. All is well. Trust me," she said and caressed her arm.

"I do," Elsie said and let out a huge puff of air once again. "I'm sorry, I am just nervous—"

"Done!" Lanora cut across her. "You are ready for your dress."

Marjory and Dorothy admired Lanora's handiwork and helped her affix their mother's diamond-studded tiara to the crown of her head. "There," Dorothy said. "You have a piece of Mama."

Elsie stood and embraced her sisters, giving each a kiss on the cheek. "You truly are the best sisters I could ask for."

Anna removed the dress from its hanger and pooled it on the floor, to make it easier for Elsie to step into. They brought it up around her hips, then fed her arms through until it was perfectly in place. Anna fastened the long row of buttons in the back, and Elsie turned to observe herself in the full-length mirror.

"My, I do look quite pretty, do I not?" she said and twirled to see herself from all angles.

"You do, indeed," came a deep voice from the doorway. At first Elsie thought it was Leo, about to bring them infinite bad luck by catching a glimpse of her before the wedding. But when she turned around she saw not Leo but Father.

Dr. Watt wheeled him into the room, and Father had a tender smile on his face. "You look so much like your mother," he said and slowly lifted his hand to brush her cheek. Elsie stepped forward and brought his hand up to her face and kissed it.

"I brought you something, darling," Father said and motioned to the package sitting on his lap.

"Oh, Father, you did not need to. You have spent so much already on the wedding—"

"It is not every day your firstborn gets married. I insist."

Elsie unwrapped the package and lifted out the most beautiful shawl she had ever seen. It was brown velvet with stunning buckles, from which hung hundreds of tiny bronze animals.

"It is beautiful, Father. Thank you."

"I wish your mama could be here to see you like this. She would be so proud."

"She is with me, today, Father. I could never do this without her."

As Elsie walked down the long, petal-strewn aisle, she felt an overwhelming sense of "Finally." In fact, she could sense it in the air, it was on the mind of each guest, even the Book Hall itself emitted the word.

The clergyman worked the word into almost every sentence of the nuptial message. "Elsie had *finally* found her soulmate." "When Leo *finally* proposed ..."

For a brief moment, Elsie considered turning around and bolting out of the hall. *Am I making a mistake?* she thought, as she tried to talk herself down. *Maybe they are right, it never should have taken this long. Does Leo even really love me, or does he merely tolerate me?*

She stole a quick glance at the audience. Her aunts dabbed at their eyes, Father looked calm and composed, and Dr. Watt's gaze traveled from the happy couple to the back of Marjory's head a full five times in that brief moment.

Does Leo look at me like that—?

Just then Leo grabbed her hands, and she noticed she had been fidgeting with the buckles on her wrap. He covered her hands with his and looked her straight in the eyes. He smiled at her, and she slowly inhaled and breathed out, clearing her lungs.

The clergyman continued his message, and when he asked her to "repeat after me," Elsie did so in full confidence. *All will be well.*

AT THE TRAIN STATION the next day, the wedding party and the few remaining guests lined the platform. Leo and Elsie waved, then kissed, then waved again, and they were off, headed to New York for a week.

Elsie felt invigorated at the thought of the approaching trip to Europe. She had not been abroad in a few years, and she found that she actually missed it. What once she had called her home now felt just exotic enough to be exciting once again.

She considered the souvenirs she would purchase for her family members, and a few for the servants. Perhaps a lovely jewelry box for Marjory, and a nice, leather-bound volume of one or other of Dorothy's favorite poets. For Father, perhaps a painting of the Italian Alps, to reside with his collection of fine art.

January 25, 1908
New York City

My dearest Marjory,

We have arrived safely in New York and leave for Italy in a few days' time. I confess I am not looking forward to the bumpy voyage across the sea, but I know it will all fade away when I am standing in front of the Parthenon, eating gelato and sipping away at a lemonade.

Would you tell Lanora thank you from me for packing my trunk with such care? She truly thought of everything. She even remembered to pack my parasol with the blue flowers on it, and also my second pair of kid gloves. I've already spoilt the first pair—oh, dear!

Please tell Father the trains were impeccable and undoubtedly up to his standards, although the final train into New York was rather dirty. Perhaps you should omit that last bit when you tell him …

I promise to write again once we've arrived in Italy.

Yours affectionately,
Els

January 28, 1908
Glen Eyrie

World traveler Elsie,

All is well here at home. Everyone misses you both. Father says to please say hello to Leo, and to tell him to mention his name when you get to Claridge's.

   Now on to more ... important ... matters. I scoured your last letter, but you so cunningly left it out. What I mean to say is, how is the "honeymoon" going? I hope you understand me when I use quotation marks in that way, for I would blush to write my real meaning.

Say hello to Italy for me,
Marj

February 14, 1908
Rome

Marjory,

Italy says hello—or should I say ciao!

   I perfectly deduce your meaning, but I cannot oblige you. Not until you are married as well, that is. Then we can write all we want about such matters. Speaking of married, when do you expect to see Wellesley again? Is he back from his tour of duty?

   Tell Father hello back from Leo, and that we intend to mention his name at Claridge's, as instructed.

Yours,
Els

February 5, 1908
Glen Eyrie

Elsie,

Marjory mentioned she had a letter from you, but she would not allow me to read it. What did it say? If it mentioned Wellesley at all, I would be most surprised. I have to tell you, Elsie, I am quite worried about our sister. She speaks less and less about Wellesley each passing day. I dared to inquire after him the other day, and she insisted all was well and the June wedding is still on.

I must say I do not believe her, though. I have found her and Dr. Watt conversing in the library or in the music room, and often without another soul present. I even saw them conversing outside her bedroom door last week, and they quickly departed the hallway as soon as they heard my footsteps. You don't think they have ... taken up with each other, do you?

Worried,
Dos

February 15, 1908
Rome

My dear Dos,

I am not surprised to hear you speak so about Wellesley, Marjory, and Dr. Watt. In fact, in my last letter to Marjory, I inquired after Wellesley, and I have yet to receive a reply. I thought perhaps she had become too busy to write, but now I feel certain she did not respond for another reason entirely: she is ashamed. Although what of, I simply cannot understand.

Why must she marry Wellesley, after all? She hardly knows the man, and although he promises to move to Colorado after the wedding, I have a hard time believing he will do any such thing. Then our beloved Marjory would be half a world away, and I could not bear it.

No, I say hurrah if Marjory is getting to know Dr. Watt. She must make up her mind soon about her engagement to Wellesley, but if I know Marjory at all, she must be sure of something before she commits to it. Keep an eye out, Dos, and don't let her become the subject of gossip among the servants. Encourage her, if you can. And whatever you do, mention none of this to Father.

Your loving sister,
Elsie

February 30, 1908
Glen Eyrie

Elsie,

Perhaps you are right, though I do not like it one bit. Marjory has promised Wellesley—does that mean nothing? And keep it from Father? I cannot agree to that. I will not broach the subject with him, but if he asks me outright, I refuse to lie. I do not like this at all.

Dorothy

February 15, 1908
Glen Eyrie

Dearest Elsie,

Dos mentioned she had a letter from you, and it reminded me that I had yet to reply to your last. Do forgive me.

How have you and Leo been these past few weeks? My, you must be headed to England soon. I cannot believe it is already almost March. Time has simply flown since your wedding, and with my own wedding approaching fast, I admit I am feeling a bit overwhelmed.

I cannot express to you how much help you have been in that department. Planning a wedding from halfway around the world is no small feat. Are you still planning to visit the church when you arrive to London? Wellesley says it is perfect, but you know men. I covet your opinion.

Please write to me afterwards and give me your honest opinion.

Father may wish to add to this letter. He is sleeping now, but I will ask him when he wakes.

Your devoted sister,
Marj

P.S. Father has asked me to relay something to you. He received a note from the Barringtons (you remember them, I'm sure). They are in London and would adore meeting you and Leo for lunch. I will include their address on a separate sheet of paper.

March 3, 1908
London

My dear, sweet Marjory,

I am writing this letter in two parts: one part for your eyes only, and one part to share with the family.

For your eyes only:
Dearest, I must confess something to you. I should have said this before I left, but I am telling you now. Do not marry Wellesley. I can tell your heart is not truly in the match. And you deserve a man that will light a fire within you. I do not believe Wellesley is that man. I will not say who I think is that man. We will leave it at that.

To share:
Hello from England! We arrived safely last Tuesday and are settled in at Claridge's. When we mentioned you, Father, they did not charge our account for the first night's stay. How generous of them.
All is well with Leo and I. In fact, all is more than well. I am with child. I have been to a respected doctor here in London, and he confirmed the fact. He expects the baby will be born in November. Leo is quite overwhelmed at the news, but I am simply ecstatic! I cannot contain my happiness! I know it is not proper to speak of such matters, but I could hardly wait until June to tell you all. Unfortunately, the unexpected news does change our plans. The doctor advises against travel of any kind, especially a long sea voyage, so we will be unable to return

home until after the baby is born.
  Love and hugs from Leo and I.

Your affectionate sister/ daughter/ niece …
Elsie

March 16, 1908
Glen Eyrie

Dear sister,

Congratulations! Ever since I read them your news, the family and servants have all been buzzing about the house. Everyone is so very excited!
  I can hardly believe the news myself, but it is so perfect. I am sad to hear you will not be able to return home until after the New Year, but it is more important for you and the baby to be healthy. Baby! I cannot express how happy I am for you, dearest sister. First a husband and now a baby.
  I thought about what you said in your last letter about Wellesley and I. I am sorry if I disappoint you, but I cannot break off the engagement. Perhaps Wellesley is a bit stiff, and perhaps he will refuse to leave England, but the truth is I love him. And I want to marry him. At least, I think I want to marry him. Oh, I don't know.
  You asked for honesty, and here it is: I cannot marry who I want to marry, so I must marry who is willing to marry me. And that person is Wellesley.

Love,
Marj

March 30, 1908
London

Marj,

Why ever do you say that? "I cannot marry who I want to marry." Do you mean who I think you mean? If so, then why can you not marry him? If you think Father will disapprove, you are wrong. Father loves him. I believe he thinks of him as a son, *and what could be more perfect than that? Wellesley is a military lieutenant; he is a doctor. This is the twentieth century, and in the twentieth century, those men are equal.*

Do not be afraid.

Lovingly,
Elsie

March 18, 1908
Orchard House

Dear niece, Elsie,

Hello from Colorado! Many congratulations on your news! I can hardly believe it. How wonderful! Drink deeply of your happiness, my dear, let it fill you up. You deserve it.

I hope you will keep me informed of your progress.

My dear, we have much to discuss. I cannot wait to see you this summer. Meanwhile, there is a matter of delicate importance we must discuss right now. It concerns Marjory. You and I have long suspected that she does not wholly love Wellesley, but now I am convinced her affections lie in another direction entirely. In Dr. Watt. Now, that would be a wonderful match. William and I are most fond of him. I have spoken with Dorothy about this matter, and she has told me of their conversations outside her bedroom door, and their whispering together by the fire. All signs point to an amore.

I am eager to know your thoughts.

Your devoted aunt,
Lottie

March 20, 1908
Glen Eyrie

Elsie,

Father asked me to dictate a letter to you. Here it is. - Dos

Darling daughter,

I am so pleased to hear about your wonderful news! I cannot wait until we have a little one running around the house again. I do so miss it.

We have begun preparations for our voyage to England. Oddly, your sister does not seem as enthusiastic about the trip as before. In fact, she often appears quite melancholy. Dorothy assures me all is well, but I do wonder. Alas, I am sure it is nothing.

I am happy to hear Claridge's is treating you with such generosity.

Love you and miss you,
Father

April 3, 1908
London

Aunt Lottie,

You are right. I have long suspected an amore between our Marjory and Dr. Watt, and Dorothy's observations only confirm it. Do what you can to encourage Marjory, will you?

Your devoted niece,
Elsie

April 4, 1908
London

Dearest Father of mine,

Thank you for the letter. I was so very happy to receive it. Thank you for the congratulations, as well. I believe I will be "showing" by the time you all arrive to London.

Father, Marjory seems her happy self in her letters to me. But might you ask her instead? I would hate to speculate.

Your devoted daughter,
Els

April 5, 1908
London

Marj,

I have not time for a long letter, but I must convey this to you. Father suspects. He wrote to me and asked me if I thought you seemed melancholy. Oh Marjory, do tell him the truth. We cannot go on like this. Dorothy is unwilling to conceal the truth from Father, and it would be better if you told him yourself lest he find out from someone else. I'm begging you.

Love,
Els

April 20, 1908
Glen Eyrie

Oh Elsie,

You do not understand. I cannot love Dr. Watt. He is the picture of health and vitality. I am weak—too weak to ride, too weak to frolic, too weak to have children. He deserves more than I can give him.

Marj

April 29, 1908
Glen Eyrie

Greetings Elsie,

I hope you and Leopold are both doing very well. We are having very pleasant weather here in Colorado. Plenty of sunshine and little rain. I am writing to you to keep you abreast of your father's improvements. He is doing very well. The warm weather and fresh air seem to agree with him.

We have a lot to prepare for our trip to England, and I admit I am still a little hesitant to allow him to travel. But I know how important it is to him, so I am determined to make it as comfortable and easy for him as possible.

We are all well here at Glen Eyrie. Your sisters have been wonderful company. Please tell Leopold a hearty hello from me.

Be well,
Watt

P.S. Marjory has been most devoted in her attentions to your father. It is admirable. She is admirable. I have never met her equal. Miss Elsie, please tell me. Do I have hope?

May 14, 1908
London

Mr. Watt,

Your letter has brought such a smile to my face! I urge you, Leo and I both urge you, to talk to Marjory. Make your feelings known to her. We would be honored to call you our brother-in-law.

Your friend,
Elsie

◆━━━━━•━━━━━◆

May 14, 1908
London

Dos,

It is official. He loves her. Darling, you must help her see she cannot marry Wellesley. She will not listen to me. It pains me to say it, but our dearest sister is about to make a big mistake. We cannot let her.

Yours,
Elsie

◆━━━━━•━━━━━◆

May 30, 1908
Glen Eyrie

Dear Elsie,

I have the most exciting news! Before you think, "It must be about Marj and Watt," let me say quickly it is not. Marj is as stubborn as ever. No, it is about me.

I have been accepted into a school in London for nurses! Dr. Watt and I have been doing lessons together for some weeks, and he also assisted me with the application. He has been a wonderful help. He even allowed me to perform all of Father's daily examinations one day, without supervision. He checked my work *afterward and declared it "the best he'd ever seen!"*

Oh Elsie, I am so very excited. The school begins in September, right after Marj's wedding. So when I leave with the party, I will not be returning to Glen Eyrie for some time. But with you and Leopold (and the baby!) living in London at least until the New Year, I will have your company to look forward to.

We leave tomorrow for New York. See you in two weeks, my sister.

Dos

MAY 31, 1908

THE BIG DAY HAD arrived. The Glen Eyrie party—Father, Dorothy, Marjory, Dr. Watt, Aunt Lottie, and Uncle William—left Colorado Springs early in the morning on a train bound for New York. When they arrived, they almost immediately boarded the *S.S. Minneapolis*, a grand steamer with a black belly and bright red smokestack. The ship reminded Dorothy of the one that had transported them from England so many years before. Who could have known then that they would one day travel back to attend Marjory's wedding?

They settled into their First-Class accommodations—Father and Dr. Watt in one suite, and Dorothy and the bride-to-be in another. Convening for dinner that evening, Dorothy paid special attention to Marjory's interactions with Watt. *Is Elsie right?* she thought. *Or is Marjory truly in love with Wellesley?*

Marjory's attitude towards Watt was aloof, disinterested, almost as if they had had a fight right before they embarked. Dorothy could not understand it, and Father did not seem to notice. Too bad she could not write to Elsie, for she needed her advice. *What do I know about love?* she thought. *Elsie is so much better at this than I am. I wish she was here.*

Dorothy spent much time debating with Aunt Lottie whether or not she should speak with Marjory about Wellesley and Watt and all the rest of it, but in the end she decided it was not her place. She could not give advice on matters in which she had no experience. Florenz was one thing, but this was real, adult, complicated love. Not a silly teenaged romance.

On the third night of the voyage, while laying wide awake in bed, Marjory spoke into the dark room, "Dos, Dos, are you awake?"

Dorothy grumbled and rolled over onto her side, away from Marjory.

"Dos!" she whispered again, louder this time. "I need to tell you something."

Dorothy rolled onto her back and slowly propped herself up on her elbows. "What is it, Marj? It's nearly three in the morning."

Marjory paused for a moment, and Dorothy could see her sister take two deep breaths before she continued, "I am not going to marry Wellesley."

Dorothy pulled back her bed covers and tiptoed over to Marjory's bed, climbed in and hugged her. Neither of them said another word. Eventually, they fell asleep and when they woke the next morning, they were still sharing a bed.

The sisters dressed for the day, with the assistance of a maid, and met Father and Watt for breakfast on the upper deck. The ship swayed gently from side to side, and the waves made a *flap-flapping* sound as they came into contact with the weathered wood. Dorothy did not speak much at breakfast, for she was deep in thought. *What does Marjory mean she will not marry Wellesley?* she thought. *And what does it mean for Dr. Watt? Oh, I wish she would say something.*

After they finished eating, Watt took Father back to his room for a short rest. Father could not handle more than an hour or two of sunlight and company without needing a break. Watt found the sisters later on the sun deck, sitting in wooden reclining chairs, their faces angled toward the sun. As he walked up, Dorothy could sense he wished to speak to Marjory alone, so she pretended to yawn and stretched out her arms.

"Goodness, I am tired, too. Must be all of this sun. You won't mind if I retire for a bit, would you, Marj?" Dorothy said.

Marjory looked at her sister then and gave her a smile of gratitude. "Not at all, dear."

MARJORY AND WATT CHATTED about the ship and the voyage, how well Father was doing, and how eager they were to see Elsie again. Soon they ran out of polite topics to discuss, and Watt let out a loud huff and leaned back in his reclining chair.

"What is it?" Marjory asked. "Tell me."

Watt did not reply for a moment and closed his eyes against the sun. He let out another loud huff, then leaned forward quickly and grabbed hold of Marjory's hand.

"Watt, I—"

"Don't say a word, Marjory," he said. "I know."

"What do you know?"

"I know you mean to call off the wedding," he replied.

"How did you—"

"It was nothing you said, really, but rather how you look. For weeks you have looked downcast, sad even. Not the normally happy woman I know and …"

"And … what?"

"Love, Miss Marjory Palmer," he said. "Know and love."

The air between them thickened under the weight of the forbidden word being spoken, after so much time. Always implied, never admitted, but once the word hit Marjory's ears, she began to laugh. A hearty belly laugh that stretched across her face and into her eyes.

"Why do you laugh?" he asked. "Have I made a fool of myself? But I was certain you felt—"

"I do, Henry, I do feel the same. And I can finally say it."

Taking her use of his Christian name as a sign of intimacy, Watt stood up and pulled Marjory to her feet, as well. He kissed her hand again gently, then lightly touched her face. He leaned in for a kiss but then pulled back slightly.

"Why do you hesitate?" she asked him.

"I have loved you for months, almost upon first meeting you. I have kept my feelings buried deep inside, but they are finally able to be set free, to breathe. It is a new sensation. I think I need a moment to collect my thoughts," he said and pulled his hand away from her face.

"Please don't," she said, grabbed hold of his hand, then leaned in and kissed him.

As he pulled away, he said nothing, only smiled.

"DOS ... DOS ... ARE YOU awake?" Marjory half-whispered into the dark room.

"Mmmmm," Dorothy responded and rolled onto her back.

"The most wonderful thing has happened."

Dorothy sat upright in the bed and rubbed her eyes. "Tell me."

"Henry, that is, Watt and I ... we're going to be married."

The words hung in the air briefly before the room fell silent. Marjory snapped on the small table lamp and looked at her sister.

"Finally!" Dorothy said and jumped up to hug her.

"Oh goodness, I thought for a moment you were mad!"

"Not at all, dear sister, not at all. Elsie and I have been waiting for this moment for weeks. I am just glad it's finally done."

"You surprise me. I knew Elsie believed I should call off my engagement with Wellesley, but I thought you were against the idea."

"Well ..." she started. "Elsie did talk me into it. But I am immensely happy for you."

Marjory burst into laughter at her sister's admission, and the pair embraced again.

Dorothy pulled back then, as if she just realized something. "How are you going to tell Father?"

Marjory's eyes widened at the thought, and she said, "I had not gotten that far."

"Don't worry," Dorothy replied, "Aunt Lottie and I will help you think of the perfect way to tell him."

THE NEXT MORNING AT breakfast, Father looked more imposing than normal—to Marjory, at least. She, Dorothy, and Aunt Lottie had spent hours the night before discussing the "big talk" she planned to have with Father. They rehearsed what she should say, what they believed Father might say, even what Watt should say. She had not had time to speak with Watt but had slipped a note under his door in the early morning hours. She hoped and prayed he had read it and agreed.

Father and Dorothy chatted merrily of the weather, the excellent time they were making, and their anticipation to see Elsie and Leo soon. When the conversation turned to the topic of Marjory's upcoming nuptials, Watt seized his chance.

"If I may, sir—"

"*Sir?* What has gotten into you, Watt, calling me 'sir'?"

Watt stole a quick sideways glance at Marjory and continued, "I do apologize, Palmer. I admit I am a bit nervous." He wrung his hands in his lap, took a deep breath, and launched into his speech.

"I am in love with your daughter, Palmer. I have loved her for months. I have not professed my love for fear you would think me impertinent. I realize my station in life is decidedly below hers, but I believe I could make her happy and provide her with a comfortable home. Please allow me to try."

Father said nothing, merely stared at Watt. Marjory could not read his facial expression. Fearing the worst, she said, "Father, I—"

"Marjory, please do not say a word. I need a moment to think. Watt, would you please take me back to my room?"

Watt stood up and grabbed hold of the handles on Father's wheelchair. He pushed him forward and disappeared down the corridor. Dorothy and Marjory watched as they left.

Dorothy let out a loud sigh, as if she had been holding her breath the whole time. She looked at Marjory, who appeared both terrified and resolved.

"He will come around," she said and picked at her breakfast. "He has to."

A few minutes later, Watt returned to their table and plopped down into a chair. "I will admit that did not go as well as I had planned."

"I suppose we could not expect more. It is the first he is hearing of it. We have had some time to get used to the idea," Marjory replied.

"You make it sound like I have resolved to dye my hair blue."

Marjory and Aunt Lottie burst into laughter at the thought of ever-professional Dr. Watt with blue locks.

ELSIE, I WISH YOU *were here*, Dorothy thought. *You would know what to say to Father.*

"You seem despondent, Dos," Marjory said as she linked arms with her sister. They had spent the last hour walking back and forth along the upper deck. Watt had retired to the card room to help relieve some stress.

"Marjory! Dorothy!" they heard a voice call out behind them and turned to see Watt sprinting up to meet them. "Your father is ready to talk."

The three hurried along back to Palmer's room, where a maid had laid tea for them. Father greeted them as they entered the room. He still wore the stern look from earlier, but his eyes were kind. No one said a word as they sipped their tea and ate their tea cake.

Father broke the silence. "I have been thinking," he said, "and I have come up with a solution that I believe will work."

"A solution? But, Father—"

"Please allow me to finish, Marjory. Wellesley is a good man, with an honest income, from a good family. He could provide you with good standing in society, trips abroad whenever you desire, fine clothes, a nice home."

Marjory bowed her head. Father cleared his throat and continued,

"But if you are the daughter I raised, I know none of that would make any difference to you."

Marjory looked up then and stared at her father.

"Watt," he said and turned his head to look at him. "You know I love you like a son. It is time you become one by law."

Marjory gasped and jumped out of her seat. She ran to Father's side and planted a big kiss on his cheek. "Thank you, Father. Thank you!"

"Now," Father said, "we must discuss the delicate matter of informing Wellesley. And minimizing the negative backlash that is sure to follow such an announcement."

THREE DAYS LATER, THEY arrived in Southampton. Elsie and Leo stood on the dock, waving as they disembarked. Dorothy, Marjory, and Aunt Lottie hugged Elsie and took turns touching her belly while Watt and Uncle William shook hands with Leo. Elsie kissed Father and asked him all about the voyage.

"Your sister has some news," he said and smiled at Marjory.

"Oh?" Elsie and Leo said in unison.

Watt put his arm around Marjory's waist and said, "We are engaged."

Elsie shouted for joy, ran up to the happy couple, and hugged and kissed them both. "I can hardly believe it! This makes me so immensely happy!"

"I, too, am so pleased with your news," Leo said, stoically.

"Now, let's get you to the hotel," Elsie said and led them through the crowd and out to the street, where the hired cars waited. Elsie had arranged a special car to transport Father. "Claridge's, please," she said.

As the cab pulled away from the curb, the Palmer girls giggled together like old times as, at Elsie's insistence, Marjory divulged the moment Watt confessed his love to her.

"Have you told Wellesley yet?" Elsie asked.

"No, I haven't. No post on the ship, remember? I hope to write to him as soon as we arrive to the hotel."

"You must excuse me. My brain has been so foggy lately, it is a wonder I even remembered you were arriving today."

"That reminds me," Dorothy said. "I wonder how long we will stay in England, now that the wedding will be called off."

"If it is up to me, you will stay until the baby is born."

Marjory received Wellesley's reply over a week later. His letter was both short and curt, which was just as expected, but she could not help feeling somewhat disappointed. He had never loved her in the proper way. It had been infatuation at first, but he showed no concern over her illness and, she believed, had no intention of living in Colorado after the wedding. Her sisters took it as proof that she had made a wise decision to call it off.

"You need a man who is humble and kind and gracious," Aunt Lottie said. "Watt is all of those things, Marjory. You made a good choice."

"Thank you," Marjory replied. "I did love Wellesley, but it was not the right kind of love. I know that now."

"I am proud of you," Dorothy said. "Your wedding day will be filled with joy."

NOVEMBER 1908
LONDON, ENGLAND

"PUSH, ELSIE, PUSH!" MARJORY coached as she grasped her sister's hand, and Dorothy laid a cool cloth on her forehead.

"Almost there," the doctor said. "Just one more big push, and it will all be over."

Moments later, the doctor said softly, "Here we are," as he laid the baby on Elsie's chest.

Elsie, still panting from the long labor, cried as she looked into the tiny face of her daughter.

The doctor cleaned Elsie, and Aunt Lottie helped her into a fresh nightgown. They bathed the baby and wrapped her tightly in a swaddling blanket.

"I will fetch Leo," Dorothy said and exited the room.

She returned with Leo in tow. Elsie reached out for his hand and said, "Meet your daughter."

He smiled then and stretched out a finger to stroke his baby's face.

"What will you call her?" Marjory asked.

Leo and Elsie looked at each other before replying, almost in unison, "Elsie Queen."

"Elsie Queen Myers Hamilton," Dorothy said. "It is a lovely name."

"Father will be so happy that you named her after Mama," Marjory said. "Will you call her 'Queen' for short, or—"

"We have discussed calling her 'EQ' for short," Elsie replied. "But what do you think, Father?" she said as Watt steered him into the room.

"It's perfect. She's perfect."

Everyone gathered around to admire baby EQ as she slept. She looked rather like a porcelain doll, with perfectly formed features and a surprising amount of thick, dark hair.

After the men left, the doctor taught Elsie how to breastfeed and about the proper care of EQ's tender skin. When he showed her how to wrap the *nappie* so as to prevent leakage, Elsie felt sad for a brief moment. Normally, a woman's mother would be the one to teach a new mother these things.

She reached out for her sisters' hands and squeezed them gently. She did not say a word, but they understood. They all missed her.

"I CANNOT BELIEVE WE are going home today," Marjory said as she held EQ in the crook of her arm. "I will miss you, little one." She bent down and kissed the top of the baby's head.

"Aye, so will I," Watt said and stroked her downy hair.

Elsie admired the way Watt took to her daughter so naturally. *He will make a wonderful father one day,* she thought.

They would leave London that day to head to Southampton. Their ship left the next morning at the stroke of six.

"Thank you all so much for your help these past two weeks," Elsie said. "It made my transition into motherhood so effortless."

Elsie chose not to employ a wet nurse for EQ; instead, she insisted on bathing and feeding her herself. Leo did not approve of her unconventional approach, but Elsie believed it would be better to do so. Mama had been uncommonly highly involved in their lives throughout their childhood, and Elsie had always admired the fact.

"I RECEIVED A LETTER from Marjory today," Elsie said as she and Leo enjoyed dinner together after a long day. "It seems Father has suffered a minor head injury."

"Gracious me, how did that happen?" Leo replied.

"Here, I will read you her letter."

Dearest Elsie,

I have some terrible news to relay. On our return voyage, Father convinced Watt to allow him to "take in the sights" from a top deck on the ship. Father's wheelchair was too cumbersome, so Watt enlisted the help of a few crew members to help lift Father in a sort of makeshift cot.

During this fool's errand, one of the crew members stumbled, and Father hit his head very hard against a railing. It knocked him unconscious, but Watt was able to revive him very quickly, thank heavens. They transported him back to his room almost immediately, whereupon Watt administered the proper care. He stayed by his bedside that entire day and into the night. We both did.

The next morning, Father said he felt fine, but we noticed he seemed very subdued. He has been lethargic and downcast ever since. I do not wish to alarm you, but I would disappoint myself if I did not say it:

Please come home.
I will write to Dos, as well.

Yours,
Marjory

"That sounds more serious than just a minor injury, darling," Leo said.

Elsie looked fear-stricken at the thought of what the injury might mean for Father's health.

Leo noticed the look on her face and said, "We will leave tomorrow. I will handle it all."

Chapter Ten

Because I could not stop for Death, He kindly stopped for me; the
carriage held but just ourselves and immortality.

EMILY DICKINSON

JANUARY 1909
GLEN EYRIE

"THEY ARE HERE!" MARJORY exclaimed to no one in particular as she
quickly descended the main staircase and entered the parlor.

Berty pulled open the large wooden door as Marjory bounded
outside to greet them. She had not stopped to put on her coat, but she
did not mind. She felt thrilled to see Dorothy, Elsie, Leo, and especially
baby EQ.

She embraced them in turn and ushered them into the warm
entryway.

"It is very nice to see you again, Berty," Elsie said as she handed him her coat.

"Sir," Leo said and nodded his head at the butler.

"Oh my dear, could it be the famous baby EQ?" Mrs. Simmons said as she approached them. "How adorable you are, *wee bairn*!" Mrs. Simmons reached out to hold the baby and Elsie obliged.

"Thank you, Missus Simmons," she said and turned to Marjory. "Is all well?"

"Father has improved somewhat over the past week," she replied, "but he becomes fatigued easily now. He takes little interest in his favorite pursuits and refuses to read."

"That is not normal at all," Dorothy replied.

"No."

They ascended the stairs to Father's room. Dorothy sat by Father's bedside as Watt sat at Father's old desk, scribbling notes into his leather-bound journal. He looked up as he heard them enter and turned to embrace Elsie and Leo.

"Who is it?" Father asked in a low, gruff voice.

"It's us, Father," Elsie replied and stepped forward. She kissed him on the cheek and sat down at the foot of his bed.

"My darling girl," he said with a smile, leaned his head back on his pillow, and briefly closed his eyes. When he reopened them, for a moment he looked quite confused, but then he said, "I am so glad you are all back. Where is my granddaughter?"

"Here she is," Mrs. Simmons said and leaned in to show Father the baby.

"My, my, she does look bigger. And so much like Queen."

"Father," Elsie said slowly, "are you alright? How are you feeling?"

"Oh, never mind about that," he replied. "I am perfectly fine."

Elsie looked at Dorothy and then at Watt, who bowed his head slightly. She could feel tears forming in the corners of her eyes and reached up a hand to brush them away.

"We should let your father rest," Watt said as he stood.

"Quite right," Leo responded and patted Elsie on the arm. They congregated in the hallway outside of Father's room.

"Tell me the truth, Watt," Elsie said. "Is he going to be alright?"

Watt paused for a moment before he replied, "It is hard to tell. I admit I had hoped he would have recovered by now, but you can see he has not."

"Father is strong," Marjory added. "He will pull through."

"His mind may be strong, but his body is not," Watt replied. "We must prepare ourselves for what will come."

THROUGHOUT EARLY WINTER, FATHER'S health wavered. He would rally for a few days but then get worse. He spent the bulk of most days in his room, resting, and guests were regularly turned away by Berty or Mrs. Simmons. Most of them left cards or small notes of encouragement, and the girls would read them to him in the evenings.

The notes always raised his spirits, as did baby EQ. She giggled and smiled and cooed, completely oblivious to the fact that her grandfather slipped away a little more each day.

On clear days, Glen Eyrie Martin brought the Steamer around to take Father on his usual joyrides. He enjoyed being out in his beloved rugged countryside.

"I have increased his morphine dosage slightly and will begin to administer a mild sedative before bed each night," Watt explained to the girls one afternoon as Father rested.

"Does he suffer?" Marjory asked with a sad look on her face.

"Not much, but he does complain of discomfort. He cannot feel most of his own body, but he has a continual headache that will not seem to lessen."

"Poor Father," Dorothy said.

MARCH 13, 1909

"DARLING," WATT SAID SOFTLY as he stroked Marjory's hair. He had crept into her bedroom in the early morning hours.

Marjory opened her eyes and looked at him. "It's Father, isn't it?"

"Let us wake the others, and I will tell you all together."

Marjory gathered Dorothy, Elsie, and Leo, and they congregated in the Book Hall, near the fire Watt had asked Lanora to light minutes earlier. Dorothy pulled her shawl tighter across her shoulders as Watt began to speak.

"Before bed last night," he began, "he complained of an intense headache and wanted to retire early. I stayed in his room all night. I sensed he might awaken in the middle of the night, and I wanted to be at hand to administer more medicine." He paused then and swallowed a couple of times.

"Go on," Elsie encouraged him.

"A bird calling outside his window woke me up around four-thirty, and I quickly realized his breathing was very shallow. I checked his pulse and listened to his heart," he explained. "I am afraid your Father is comatose."

Dorothy began to cry softly, and her sisters gathered around to embrace her. They remained that way for some time, crying and praying. As they pulled away, Watt and Leo stepped forward and hugged them each in turn.

"I suppose we should tell Berty and Missus Simmons," Elsie said after a few moments.

"Leave that to me," Leo replied and left the room in search of the pair.

The Palmer girls sat by their father's side the entire day. They stroked his hair, told him how much they loved him, and watched as he took his final breath that afternoon.

Watt rose slowly from his chair and checked the great man's pulse. He placed a small mirror against his chin to check his breathing. His shoulders drooped, and he turned around to face the girls. "He has gone home to be with the Lord."

After an hour, Watt left the room in search of the telephone to make arrangements for the transportation of Palmer's body to a place in town. Before his passing, Palmer had given Watt very specific instructions on how he wanted things to happen. He had not wanted to burden his daughters in their time of grief.

"He looks like he is sleeping," Dorothy remarked.

"He does," Elsie agreed and leaned in to stroke his cold cheek.

Marjory pulled a small Quaker prayer book from Father's bedside table and opened it to where a bookmark marked his favorite passage:

I pray for faith, I long to trust.
I listen with my heart, and hear
A Voice without a sound: "Be just,
Be true, Be merciful, revere
The Word within thee: God is near!"

MARCH 17, 1909
COLORADO SPRINGS

"WE COULD NOT HOPE for a more beautiful day," Elsie said to Leo as she admired the warm weather. "Father loved days like these."

Elsie, Dorothy, Marjory, Leo, and Watt rode in Father's beloved car, while Aunt Lottie and Uncle William followed behind in their own car. They drove into town, and Leo pointed out how quiet it was—no train whistles, no car horns, no sounds of children playing in the schoolyard. Even the flags were flown at half-staff.

As they approached Evergreen Cemetery, they saw an enormous crowd gathered. Thousands of townspeople, Colorado College students, family, and friends were there to honor the beloved General Palmer. Father had chosen his burial plot years before and commissioned a headstone made of a red boulder from Ute Pass. It was a truly serene and lovely bit of land.

Reverend Arthur Taft performed the funeral service, after which the mayor of Colorado Springs got up to speak, describing Palmer as "the soldier, the builder of an empire, the philanthropist, the friend of the people, whose life was a blessing." The Palmer girls clasped hands as they stepped forward to toss the first bit of dirt onto their father's grave.

"We love you, Father," Elsie said.

"We miss you dearly," Dorothy chimed in.

"We will never forget you," Marjory added.

Several others stepped forward then and tossed more dirt onto the grave. Some said brief prayers, and others read bits of Scripture.

BACK AT GLEN EYRIE, Palmer's closest friends and family gathered to eat lunch and pay their respects to the family.

As the day wore on and the guests began to leave, Leo noticed the girls were missing from the group. He went in search of them and found them in the Book Hall, sitting cross-legged on the floor in front of the fire, with several large photograph albums open before them. They spoke of their mother and their father, and smiled tenderly as they swapped stories.

Leo joined their little circle and pulled one album close to him. Elsie turned and pointed out a photo of Mama sitting on the stone bridge near the castle entrance. She wore a white dress and a serene look.

"This is my favorite one of our mama. She looked happy there," Elsie remarked. "Before her illness and our move to England. The whole world was before her. She could not know then how things would change."

"We cannot alter the past," Dorothy said and placed a hand over her sister's. "All we can do is take the good things and move forward, whatever may come."

Elsie smiled broadly at her. "You are right. You are absolutely right. Come, let us be happy."

The End

EPILOGUE

AFTER PALMER'S DEATH, Elsie, Leo, and baby EQ continued to live at Glen Eyrie for several months before returning to England permanently in 1910. That year, Elsie gave birth to their second daughter, Eveleen Hamilton Myers. She was named after Leo's mother, Eveleen Tennant. Tragically, Leo died in 1944 by suicide. Elsie died in 1955 at the age of 83.

DOROTHY ATTENDED NURSING school and became a social worker, spending many years devoted to welfare work in the slums of London. She never married. She traveled the world with painter Lawrence Alexander Harrison and his wife, Alma, and painter John Singer Sargent. She died in 1961 at the age of 81.

SHORTLY AFTER MARRYING, Marjory and Dr. Watt moved to a house on Culebra Avenue in the heart of Colorado Springs. They could not have children but instead devoted their lives to caring for those with tuberculosis and founded Sunniest Sanitorium in Colorado Springs. Dr. Henry C. Watt died in 1917 at the age of 45. After his death, Marjory turned their house into a camp for undernourished children. She returned to England a few years later and died from tuberculosis complications in 1925 at the age of 44.

CHARLOTTE AND WILLIAM Sclater moved to England shortly after the death of Palmer. In 1942, Charlotte died from injuries she sustained during the bombing of London. Two years later, William died after a V-1 flying bomb fell over his home.

THROUGH WILLIAM JACKSON Palmer's unfailing devotion to his beloved Colorado Springs, it has become a city of much beauty. To this day, around town you can see many landmarks that bear his name: Palmer Hall at Colorado College, Palmer Park, General William J. Palmer High School, and Palmer Lake, among others. He also donated land to the city to create eight spectacular parks, the Union Printer's Home, the Colorado School for the Deaf and Blind, Cragmor Sanitorium, Colorado College, and countless churches. He was a man of many talents, a clear vision, and a huge heart.

ABOUT THE AUTHOR

Ashley Eiman is a professional editor and writer living in Colorado Springs. She loves *Downton Abbey*, country music, and all things Jane Austen. This is her first novel.

Visit her website: AshleyEimanCreative.com

Contact her: AshleyEimanCreative@gmail.com